They heard some noise and knew what it was—at least, Clint and Bass knew. The men inside had tossed over some tables to use as cover.

Reaves looked at Clint, who nodded. They each knew what their moves were going to be once they were inside. Since Clint had already been in the saloon he was able to describe it for Reaves, who now knew what the inside looked like as if he'd been there himself. Bar to the left, tables to the right. Clint was going to go in and left, using the bar for cover. Reaves was going in and right, turning over a table for his own cover . . .

Reaves and Clint mounted the boardwalk and edged their way to the bat-wing doors.

"One . . ." Reaves said.

"Two . . . Clint said.

They both said "Three!" at the same time, and went into the saloon . . .

THE GUNSMITH

202

VIGILANTE JUSTICE

J. R. ROBERTS

JOVE BOOKS, NEW YORK

VIGILANTE JUSTICE

A Jove Book / published by arrangement with
the author

PRINTING HISTORY
Jove edition / November 1998

The Penguin Putnam Inc. World Wide Web site address is
http://www.penguinputnam.com

ISBN: 0-515-12393-5

A JOVE BOOK®
Jove Books are published by The Berkley Publishing Group,
a member of Penguin Putnam Inc.,
375 Hudson Street, New York, New York 10014.
JOVE and the "J" design are trademarks belonging to
Jove Publications, Inc.

PRINTED IN THE UNITED STATES OF AMERICA

10 9 8 7 6 5 4 3 2 1

THE GUNSMITH
202
VIGILANTE JUSTICE

ONE

Wade Miller had never seen a black man wearing a badge before—and certainly not a black man as fearsome-looking as Bass Reaves.

Reaves was the first black to ever be appointed a federal marshal by the famed "Hanging" Judge Parker. That was almost eight years ago, and he'd been one of Parker's best marshals ever since. He'd brought more men with prices on their heads back from Indian Territory than any other man, and Parker had long since given up trying to get Bass Reaves to bring them all back alive. After all, all he did was hang them, anyway.

Reaves had been tracking Miller through Indian Territory for weeks. Finally, he'd found him in the town of Shadow Wells. Reaves had received some information from some of his Creek Indian contacts that Miller was there. He was the only marshal the Oklahoma Native Americans would talk to, because he was the only one who wasn't a white man.

Once he got to Shadow Wells it was just a matter of time before he found Wade Miller.

Miller had been in the whorehouse for some time, in the company of a prostitute named Molly McCoy. Molly was a red-haired Irish gal with freckles on the bridge of her nose and in that valley between her small but firm breasts. Miller had spent a lot of time inspecting those freckles very closely, and now Molly was sitting astride him, riding him for all he was worth. Miller watched with fascination while her breasts bobbed about as she bounced up and down on him. She had big nipples for a girl with such small breasts, and he played with them, squeezing them and pinching them between his fingers. Finally, he couldn't hold back any longer and when she came down on him and began grinding herself on him he exploded, bellowing like a wounded bull as he emptied into her.

"Just leave the money on the table," Molly told him. He wasn't much in the looks department, she thought, but he had sure lasted a lot longer than most of the regular customers from town. He had red hair—which, she thought, was probably why he'd picked her—and he was tall and skinny with a prominent Adam's apple. Her preference—when it came to picking a man for her own pleasure—was for someone a little beefier—not fat, but certainly muscular. Still, he hadn't been bad at all. . . .

"Come back and see me again before you leave town." She made her tone sound inviting. After ten years of doing this she knew how to talk to men.

"I'll do that," Wade Miller said. "Count on it."

He dropped the money on the dresser top and left the room. He put his vest on while he walked downstairs and had his gun belt over his shoulder as he stepped outside.

That was when he saw Marshal Bass Reaves.

Reaves found out from the hotel clerk that he had given Miller directions to the town cathouse. He decided to let the man have his ride, and just wait outside for him to finish. He could see through the glass on the front door when Miller came down the steps, and he stepped out into the street to wait for him.

Miller came out of the door with his gun belt over his shoulder and stopped when he saw Reaves—and the badge on his chest.

"Led me a merry chase, Miller," Reaves said, "but I ain't chasin' you no more."

"You're . . . Bass Reaves?"

"That's right."

Miller had heard all the stories about Marshal Reaves and how he preferred to bring men back dead—especially white men. For a minute, Miller thought about his gun.

"Don't even think about that, Miller," Reaves said. "You'd never get to it in time. Jes' let that gun belt slide to the ground."

Miller didn't react right away. He was still wondering if he'd be able to get his gun out in time.

"If I drop my gun," he said, "you'll shoot me."

"That's foolish talk," Reaves said. "If you drop your gun belt why'd I wanna shoot you?"

"You always kill the men you hunt," Miller said, "especially white men."

"Is that what you've heard about me?"

"Everybody's heard it."

"Well, everybody's wrong," Reaves said. "I remember one time I didn't have to kill a man to bring him in—but he was the only one who done what I told him when I said to drop his gun . . . like I'm tellin' you now."

Miller bit his lip. He was trying to decide which way he wanted to die, going for his gun or unarmed.

" 'Sides," Reaves said, "I ain't after you."

"You ain't?" Miller seized on this piece of information like a drowning man.

"Nope."

"Who you after, then?"

"Webb," Bass Reaves said, "I want Jim Webb."

"Oh, Jesus," Miller said. "I could let you kill me now, or let Webb kill me later. That ain't much of a choice."

" 'Pears to be the only choice you got, Miller," Bass Reaves said, "and you got exactly ten seconds to make it."

TWO

It had been a while since Clint Adams had been to Fort Smith. The town hadn't changed much, still busy and dusty, much of the dust kicked up *because* it was busy. There seemed to always be wagons or horses on the streets, at least until dark. It didn't look as if any new buildings had been erected since he'd last been there, but as he passed the building that housed the jail he saw that the gallows outside had been updated. Judge Isaac Parker certainly didn't want his gallows timbers rotting away. It would be embarrassing to drop an outlaw or two through the trapdoor and have the timbers break, so every so often he had them torn down and rebuilt with new timber. Clint imagined he could almost smell the newness of this particular gallows.

In size it remained the same, however. At twenty feet long it was large enough to accommodate a dozen convicted killers, and often did.

He left Duke in the livery and walked with his rifle and saddlebags to the nearest hotel. He wasn't picky about where he stayed in Fort Smith. The hotels were all busy, and for that reason the rooms were always clean. He checked in, put his belongings in his room, and went in search of a meal. It occurred to him that the first hour or so after arriving in any town was about the same. The livery, the hotel, a meal, maybe a drink after that. Until all those things were taken care of, you could almost be in any town, anywhere.

Except maybe Fort Smith. There were more men with badges walking around Fort Smith, because Judge Parker gave them out like candy. Some of the men wearing badges used to be chased by men wearing badges, but Judge Parker claimed that these men were his best marshals. "They can think from both sides of the badge."

Judge Isaac Parker had two hundred deputy marshals working beneath him, and because of the dangerous nature of the Indian Territory these men often rode in pairs or groups. As old habits die hard, they often even walked the streets that way. Clint had known many of Parker's marshals off and on over the past eight or nine years since Parker had been assigned to the Indian Territory. The men he passed on the street this day, however, were all strangers to him. Of course, the one man who never changed, and was never a stranger, was Parker himself. Clint had met him soon after Parker was assigned to the Territory, soon after he took up residence and office in Fort Smith, Arkansas, which was judicial headquarters for the Indian Territory. Parker had wanted Clint as one of his deputies, but Clint had refused. The two men had become friends, however, and it was in response to a summons from Parker that Clint was now in Fort Smith.

Clint found a café he might have remembered from a previous trip to Fort Smith. As he was eating he realized he'd have to wait hours before he could see the judge. Parker's court session began at eight A.M. each day and went on until he decided he'd had enough.

The tables around him were all taken, and it seemed that deputy marshals sat at half of them. Clint wondered why so many of the men were in town today. He was used to seeing them around, but not in this number. Either they were remaining in town for a reason, or Parker had hired twice as many since the last time Clint was there.

Clint decided after his meal that he would present himself at the judge's office and speak to the man's clerk. If Parker wanted to see him badly enough, maybe he'd recess early once he knew Clint was there.

The clerk was not the same man who had worked there a few years earlier, when Clint was last at the judge's office.

"Can I help you?"

"Are you Judge Parker's clerk?" Clint asked.

"Yes, I have that privilege," the fussy little man said. "My name is Savage, Frederic Savage."

Clint couldn't imagine a man looking less like his name.

"Well, my name is Clint Adams, Mr. Savage, and the judge asked me to come by."

"Yes, of course, Mr. Adams," Savage said. He wore wire-framed spectacles and had a small, neatly trimmed mustache. He was impeccably dressed and smelled of something that might indicate that he'd just been to a barber. "I am aware that the judge sent for you."

"He didn't send for me," Clint said. "He asked me to come by. You see, the judge and I are friends."

"Yes, of course," Savage said, "I did not mean to imply differently. I will tell the judge that you've arrived. What hotel are you staying at?"

"The Fremont."

Savage wrote that down and seemed to wrinkle his nose at Clint's choice of hotel. Clint wanted to say something, but decided to let it go.

"I don't know when the judge will be recessing—"

"I'm aware of the judge's habits," Clint said. "I just wanted to let him know that I arrived."

"Very good," Savage said. "I will let him know."

"Fine, thanks."

Clint left Isaac Parker's office with a thorough dislike for the judge's clerk.

THREE

Clint went from the judge's office to the nearest saloon, which happened to be the biggest one in town. Over the door was a sign that said simply: NO. 5. Clint was used to seeing saloons with numbers rather than names in towns like Leadtown and other mining towns, but not in a town like Fort Smith. It also reminded him that Jim Hickok had been killed in the No. 10 Saloon in Deadwood. He went in anyway.

He walked to the bar and ordered a beer. Turning to lean against the bar while he drank the beer, he saw a table of deputy marshals who were enjoying a beer together. There were about five of them, and he didn't know four of them. The fifth one spotted him and came walking over. His name was Page.

"Clint Adams," Page said. "Haven't seen you in years."

"Page, how are you?"

The two men shook hands.

"What brings you to Fort Smith?"

"The judge."

"He sent for you?"

"He asked me to come, and I came," Clint said.

"I thought he got tired a long time ago of trying to pin a badge on you."

"I doubt that's what he has in mind."

"What do you think he has—oh, wait a minute."

"What is it?"

"I just thought—well, maybe I hadn't ought to say anything until you talk to the judge."

"Come on, Page," Clint said. "You started to say something, you might as well finish it."

"Well . . . I was just thinking that this might be about Bass Reaves."

"Bass Reaves," Clint repeated. He knew who Reaves was, the only black man Parker had ever pinned a badge on. "You know, in all the years I've been to Fort Smith he's never been here when I was."

"Bass is hardly ever here," Page said, "unless it's to come in and claim a reward."

Parker's marshals weren't paid. They received mileage, fees, and rewards when they were offered.

"Is he here now?"

"No," Page said, "he's not, and that might be what Parker wants to see you about."

"Why?"

"Well . . . Reaves has sort of been off his rocker, lately."

"Come again?"

"Off his—"

"I know what that means," Clint said. "I just wanted you to explain it."

"Well, he's got it into his head that he's got to bring back this feller Jim Webb. Have you heard of Webb?"

"Can't say I have."

"You been in the territories lately?"

"No."

"That's why, then," Page said. "Webb's been cuttin' a swath through the territories and Bass don't much like the idea."

"What's that got to do with me and Judge Parker?"

"Parker wants Reaves to come in," Page said, "and he won't."

"So?"

"So he might be wantin' you to go after him and bring him back."

"Why wouldn't he just send a couple of you fellas?"

"Because of this," Page said, tapping his badge. "You see, none of us is about to go out after a man who's wearin' one of these."

"I see."

"The judge threatened us with dismissal, but when we all refused he couldn't very well fire the lot of us. So maybe that's why he sent—uh, he asked you to come. He's gonna ask you to go after Bass."

"Reeves is the black marshal, right?"

"That's right."

"Why would you all refuse? I mean, he wasn't asking you to hunt Reaves down and arrest him, was he?"

"It don't matter why he wants Reaves brought in," Page said. "None of us are gonna hunt another man wearing a badge. That's all there is to it."

Clint frowned. He knew there was no way Parker could legally get him to go after Bass Reaves, but if he asked him to do it as a favor he didn't know how he was going to refuse. Then again, maybe Page was wrong. Maybe that wasn't why Parker had asked Clint to come to Fort Smith.

"I might be wrong," Page said.

"I was just thinking—and hoping—the same thing. What kind of man is Reaves?"

"A hard man," Page said, "harder still, probably, because he's black. He has to live up to the badge twice as much as the rest of us."

"And this Jim Webb?"

"He's a bad one," Page said. "He's already killed two marshals, and one of them was a friend of Bass."

"So that's why he wants him so bad?"

"Yeah," Page said, "and the judge don't like his marshals to have personal feelings about their jobs."

Clint was about to comment when he saw Savage, the judge's clerk, come into the saloon.

"Well," he said, "maybe I'm about to find out what the judge wants."

"I hope he don't send you after Bass, Clint," Page said. "If he does, I think one of you fellas ain't gonna come back."

FOUR

Judge Isaac Parker hadn't changed much, except possibly to have gotten even more barrel-chested. As he stood from behind his desk to greet Clint, he seemed to fill the room.

"Clint Adams, by God! Am I glad to see you, sir!" he boomed.

Clint advanced to the desk and allowed Parker to mangle his hand.

"Sit down, man!" Parker invited. Even his invitations tended to sound like commands, though. He was used to dominating a room, whether it was a courtroom full of people or simply one man in his office. "Brandy?"

"Why not?"

Although they were very close in age, Clint always felt as if he was in the presence of an older man, one who commanded respect.

"I called a short recess as soon as I heard you were here," Parker said, pouring two snifters full of good brandy. "I should string Savage up for not telling me sooner, though."

He handed Clint a brandy and then sat down behind his desk.

"You look well."

13

"You look prosperous."

Parker touched his face and said, "It's the extra weight, I know. My wife, the good woman, has been after me to lose it."

"How is she?" For the life of him Clint couldn't remember her name.

"She's fine, and still a saint for putting up with me, the good woman."

All Clint had ever heard Parker call his wife was "the good woman."

"I suppose you're wondering why I asked you to come to Fort Smith?"

"I was thinking about it, yes."

Parker checked his pocket watch.

"I'll have to blurt it out, then," he complained. "I don't have much time."

Clint knew that Parker would take as much time as he needed, and it wouldn't bother him in the least to keep a courtroom of people waiting.

"Do you know who Bass Reaves is?"

Clint released the breath he'd been holding. He'd been hoping not to hear that name during their conversation.

"I know it."

Parker read something in Clint's tone, or his countenance.

"Someone's told you, already," Parker said. "Who was it, by God? I'll string him up!"

"Somebody made a guess," Clint said. "I see it was a good one."

"Let me explain," Parker said, and went on to tell Clint everything that Page had already told him.

"Why me, Judge?" he asked.

"Because you're the best man for the job."

"Meaning?"

"Meaning you have the best chance of coming back alive, with Reaves in tow. I don't know what ever possessed me to pin a badge on the man, but, by God, he's been one of my best men for years. Now's he gone off half-cocked and he won't come back without Jim Webb.''

"Don't you want Webb?"

"I want Reaves more," Parker said. "I can't have one of my marshals running around out there out of control."

"Is he out of control?"

Parker finished his brandy and set his empty glass down on his desk.

"I don't know," he said finally. "I hear reports. He's tracking down men who might tell him where Webb is. Some of them he's . . . forcing the information out of, others are talking in return for being let go."

"I see."

"Do you? He could have come back half a dozen times with a wanted man in tow—men with prices on their heads. Instead he's bargaining with them for their freedom." Parker brought his fist down on his glass, causing his glass to jump off the desk and shatter on the floor. "I won't have that! I can't have it."

"Judge," Clint said, "the glass—"

"Damn the glass. I'll have Savage clean it up. Clint, you have to help me. I'm asking you for a favor."

There was the other word Clint hadn't wanted to hear during their conversation.

"Judge—"

"Don't say it," Parker said, holding up his hand. "I know it's unfair of me to put this in the form of a favor. Let me try to explain."

Clint remained silent.

"I have high regard for this man, Bass Reaves," Parker said. "I don't want him to ruin his career, and his life, by going off half-cocked like this."

Clint was surprised. He had thought the judge was worried about the good name of his office; he seemed to actually care about Bass Reaves as a man.

"Will you help me?"

"You know I will, Judge," Clint said.

"Excellent!" He slapped the desk with the palm of his hand this time. It did considerably less damage. "I knew I could count on you."

"You'll have to give me some idea where he is," Clint said. "I'll need a place to start."

"I've been tracking him through reports," Parker said, standing up. "I have to get back to court, but Savage will give you the information you need."

He came around the desk and extended his hand again. Clint stood and accepted it.

"I can't tell you how much I appreciate this, Clint."

"I'll do my best for you, Judge."

"I know you will, Clint," Parker said. "You're the one man I knew I could count on."

As Parker left his office Clint wasn't sure if that much confidence was a blessing, or a curse.

FIVE

Clint went out to talk to Savage and get whatever information he had.

"I've written everything down for you," the fussy little man said. "These are the last three places we heard Reaves was seen."

"Tell me something, Mr. Savage," Clint said, putting the slip of paper the man had given him into his pocket. "What do you think of Bass Reaves?"

"I really shouldn't give my opinion."

"Why not?"

"Well . . . the judge never asks for it."

"I'm asking for it. How long have you worked for the judge?"

"Eight months."

"And you've come into contact with Reaves?"

"Well . . . yes."

"And the other marshals?"

"Of course."

"Then you must have formed an opinion."

"I have."

"Then I'd like to hear it."

"Well . . . I think the same thing about Bass Reaves that I think about all the judge's marshals."

"Really? And what's that?"

The man hesitated, then cleared his throat and said, "They're barbarians, with no regard for the law they're supposed to uphold. Most of them are no better than the men the judge sentences to hang."

"And do any of them know you feel this way?"

"No!" Savage said, then his eyes widened. "You're not going to tell them, are you?"

"Of course not," Clint said. "This conversation is just between you and me."

"Thank you."

"Tell me something else."

"If I can."

"How do you rate Bass Reaves's abilities? I mean, if I'm going to be tracking him I'd like to know what I'm up against."

"Well," Savage said, looking pleased at being asked, "I would have thought you'd ask some of his fellow marshals."

"I intend to," Clint said, "but since he's one of them they might not want to answer me."

"Oh, he's not one of them."

"He's not? But he wears a badge."

"Well, he wears a badge like them, but none of them consider him to be one of them because . . . well, because of his color." Savage had lowered his voice, as if someone might hear him.

"It was my understanding that none of them would go after him."

"That was out of respect for the badge," Savage said, "not the man."

"None of them respect him?"

"Not as a man," Savage said.

"But as a deputy marshal?"

"They respect him . . . and fear him."

"Do you fear him?"

"Oh, yes," Savage said. "He's a huge brute of a man, uneducated, at the mercy of his temper."

"And the judge?"

"What about him?"

"How do he and Reaves get along?"

"Famously," Savage said. "The judge feels that Bass Reaves is, in many ways, his best man."

"And how does Reaves feel about Judge Parker?"

"He respects him."

"And likes him?"

"I don't know if Reaves likes any white man," Savage said, "but if he does, it's probably Judge Parker."

"And do you like Judge Parker, Mr. Savage?"

"I work for the judge," Savage said. "It is not necessary for me to like him."

"I see."

"You won't tell him I said that, will you?"

"Like I said," Clint repeated, "this is all just between you and me."

"Thank you, again," Savage said. "Oh, I have something for you."

Savage took an envelope out of his desk and handed it to Clint.

"What's this?"

"Expense money."

"From Judge Parker?" Clint asked, surprised. Parker was notoriously tight with a dollar.

"Yes, he felt you might have to take a train for a part of your trip, in order to catch up with Reaves."

"He might be right," Clint said. "Tell the judge I said thanks."

"You didn't discuss this?"

"No."

Savage looked unhappy. Clint wondered how honest the judge's clerk was. If he'd known that Clint and Parker hadn't discussed expenses, would he have still forked the money over?

"When will you be leaving to go after Reaves?" Savage asked.

"Probably in the morning," Clint said. "I'll use the rest of the day to talk to some of the other marshals about him."

"Well," Savage said, "I wish you luck, Mr. Adams. You're going to need it."

SIX

Before talking to the other marshals Clint went to find his friend Marshal Page again. Page had a room in one of Fort Smith's rooming houses and that's where Clint found him.

"Let's not talk here," Page said. "This room's not even big enough for one person, let alone two."

"I'll buy you a beer, then."

"What are we waiting for?"

They went back to the same saloon they'd talked in earlier. Although it was busy they managed to find a table in the back of the room. Clint noticed there weren't as many men with badges present as there had been earlier.

"What's on your mind?" Page asked.

"I met with the judge and it was just as you guessed," Clint said. "He asked me to go after Bass Reaves."

"And what did you say?"

"What else could I say? He asked me to do it as a favor."

"So now you want to know about Bass, huh?"

"I'm going to talk to some of the other marshals as well, Page, but I wanted to talk to you first."

"I can tell you about Bass."

21

"I want you to tell me about the other marshals."

"What about them?"

"Will they talk to me about Bass?"

"I don't see why not."

"Somebody indicated to me that they didn't really count Reaves as one of them because of his color. Is that really true?"

"You been talkin' to that weasel, Savage."

"I'm not going to say who told me—"

"You don't have to. It was him."

Clint remained silent.

"Okay, it's like this," Page said. "A lot of the others don't like Bass 'cause he's black, that's true. Everybody's got respect for his abilities, though."

"Including you?"

"Hell, yes," Page said. "Bass is a helluva man to have with you when things go bad, Clint. He's saved my life more times than I can count."

"Are you friends?"

"No," Page said, "but it's not because I ain't tried. To tell you the truth, I don't think Bass knows how to have friends."

"Because you and the others are white?"

"White or black," Page said. "You ever worked with a black man?"

"I have," Clint said, thinking about his friend Fred Hammer, whom he hadn't seen in years.

"You trust him?"

"With my life."

"Like him?"

"Yes."

"Consider him a friend?"

"I don't *consider* him a friend," Clint said. "He *is* a friend."

"And does he feel the same way?"

"He does."

"About anybody else but you?"

"He's got a few friends, but not a lot," Clint admitted.

"Any of them black?"

"Not that I know of."

"Bass don't seem to know how to act around people, black or white—not unless he's huntin' them."

"I understand he likes the judge."

"Savage again," Page said. "He respects the judge, but I don't know that he likes him."

"The judge seemed pretty concerned about Reaves."

"And why not? He's one of his best men."

"Page," Clint said, "is Reaves going to let me get close enough to talk to him?"

"To tell you the truth, Clint," Page said, "I don't know what's goin' on in Reaves's head right now."

"Is he good with a gun?"

"Good enough," Page said. "Not as fast as you, but accurate. Good with a rifle, too—and with his hands. I don't know any man who's ever gone up against Bass without a weapon who didn't get knocked cold. Bass Reaves is a big man, Clint, and powerful. I wouldn't advise ever tryin' to go up against him bare-handed."

"Thanks for the advice."

"He can ride a horse and read sign like an Indian, too," Page said. "Best I ever saw at trackin' a man."

"Then I wonder how much luck I'll have trackin' him," Clint said.

"Probably won't be hard," Page said. "The way I hear it, he's not makin' any secret of his passing, wherever he goes. He wants Jim Webb to know that he's after him."

"What do we know about Webb?"

"About what we know about Bass," Page said. "He's a tough man, good with a gun and a knife. He may or may not have some men with him when Bass finds him."

"And you think Bass will find him?"

"Oh yeah," Page said over the rim of his beer mug. "Bass Reaves has never not brought back a man he was tracking, Clint. He'll keep at it until he does find him."

"I guess I'd better talk to some of the others and then turn in early," Clint said. "I'm going to head out at first light."

"I'll come with you, then," Page said. "You'll want somebody to introduce you so they'll talk to you."

"I appreciate that, Page," Clint said. Both men stood up, preparing to leave. "What are my chances of convincing you to come with me when I leave in the morning?"

"Not good at all," Page said with a smile and a pat on the back.

"Just thought I'd ask," Clint said.

SEVEN

Page took Clint around and introduced him to some of the other marshals. His reception was about half-and-half, and he had a feeling that the half that did talk to him only did it because of Page. What he found out, though, was nothing new. Bass Reaves was a bad man, they said, and none of them would have wanted the job of hunting him down—not even just to give him a message from the judge.

Page left him on his own after some of the introductions, asking some of the others to continue with them. One man didn't seem to mind doing that. His name was Al Maxim.

Maxim looked to be in his early thirties, and unlike the other marshals he seemed impressed with Clint's reputation. He was willing to take Page's place for a while and introduce Clint around, but Clint had to pay the price of answering countless questions.

"Are you gonna be one of the judge's deputies now?" Maxim asked.

"No," Clint said, "I'm just doing this as a favor for the judge."

"Are you and Judge Parker friends?"

"Yes, we are."

"Wow," Maxim said.

"That impresses you?"

"It surprises me," Maxim said. "I didn't know the judge had any friends."

Finally, Clint spoke to all of the marshals who would speak to him.

"I appreciate your help, Al," he said to Maxim. "I guess you can go back to doing what you were doing."

"I wasn't doing nothin'," Maxim said. "I'm just waitin' on an assignment from the judge. Uh, could we talk about somethin'?"

"Sure," Clint said. "What's on your mind?"

"Let's go to the saloon," Maxim said. "It'd be a real pleasure if you would let me buy you a drink."

"Okay, Al," Clint said, "let's go."

They went to the same saloon Clint and Page had been in, but Clint didn't see Page around.

"He's got a woman in town," Maxim said when Clint mentioned this. "When he's waitin' for an assignment he spends time with her."

"Sounds like a good way to spend time," Clint said.

There were no tables available so Maxim and Clint stood at the bar with their beers. Maxim had said he was buying, but Clint didn't see any money change hands between the marshal and the bartender.

"What's on your mind, Al?"

"I was wonderin'," Maxim said, "if you would want me to go with you when you go after Reaves?"

"Why would you want to do that?" Clint asked. "I thought none of the marshals wanted to go after him."

"They don't."

"But you do?"

"Well, not really."

"Then what did you have in mind?"

"I'd consider it watchin' your back," Maxim said, "and not goin' after Bass."

"I see."

"You could use somebody to watch your back, couldn't you, Clint?"

Clint frowned. He could use somebody to watch his back while he was searching through the territories for Bass Reaves, but he preferred to have someone he knew he could count on. He didn't know Al Maxim from a hole in the ground, and he wasn't willing to accept the man based on the fact that Parker had made him a deputy marshal.

"I'm offerin' you my help," Maxim said. "Bein' friends with the judge, you could arrange it."

Here was Clint's out. He could always blame Parker for not letting Maxim go along.

"Let me talk to the judge in the morning, Al," he said, "and see what I can do."

That answer seemed to satisfy Maxim.

"I'd appreciate it," he said. "It would be an honor to ride with you."

"Well . . . thanks."

"And I'd pull my weight," Maxim went on. "I can shoot and track as well as any of the others, and I know my way around the territories."

If all of that was true—or even most of it—then the younger man would be an asset to him—but Clint didn't know how much the man was saying was brag, and how much was actual fact.

"I believe you, Al," Clint said. "Like I said, it'll be up to the judge."

"Get you another beer?" Maxim asked.

"No, thanks," Clint said. "I'm kind of bushed. I just rode in today, you know. I think I'll just go back to my hotel."

"I could come by in the morning—" Maxim started to say, but Clint stopped him by putting his hand on the man's shoulder.

"Al," he said, "I'll talk to the judge in the morning

and then find you and let you know what he said. For now, I'll say good night."

"Oh . . . well, okay, then," Maxim said reluctantly. "Good night, Clint. I can call you Clint, can't I?"

"You can call me—yes, you can call me Clint." He'd been about to say that Maxim could call him anything he wanted, but he didn't want to sound short with the man. He was, after all, offering his help when no one else would—not even Page, who was supposed to be a friend.

"See you in the morning, Al," Clint said, and left the saloon.

EIGHT

In the morning Clint presented himself at Judge Parker's office early enough to catch the man before his court began its session. His clerk, Savage, wasn't even in the office yet.

"I thought you'd be off with first light," Parker said, as Clint entered his office.

"I have a question for you," Clint said, seating himself in front of Parker's desk.

"About what?"

"One of your men."

"Which one?"

"Maxim."

"My newest deputy."

"How new?"

"Several months. Why?"

"He wants to go with me, to watch my back."

"I'm not surprised."

"Why not?"

"He wanted to go after Reaves on his own."

"Why didn't you let him?"

"He's too inexperienced, too young."

"He's not that young."

29

"He looks thirty," Parker said, "but he's only twenty-five."

"Why would you pin a badge on a man that young?" Parker shrugged.

"I had an extra."

"Then why not let him go after Reaves?" Clint asked. "After all, he's not hunting him like a wanted man. He'd just be delivering a message."

"First of all he'd never find him," Parker said. "Second, he'd get himself killed."

"By Reaves?"

"Before he ever got to Reaves," Parker said. "He hasn't gone on an assignment alone yet. He's not ready for that. In fact, going along with you would be good for him."

"And what about me?"

"Well, you could use someone to watch your back."

"Is he capable enough for that?"

"He's capable enough . . ."

"Yes," Clint said, pursuing the matter, "but enough to watch my back?"

Parker leaned both hands on his desk, almost looming over the seated Clint.

"He'd learn a tremendous amount from you, Clint," Parker said, "and by the time he got back here I'd have a better deputy."

"So you want me to take him."

Parker stood up straight.

"As long as he volunteered, why not?"

Why not, indeed? Clint thought. If not just for the company. Also, two men traveling together would not present such an easy supposed target as one. Having him along might save Clint a fight or two.

"All right," Clint said, standing. "I'll take him along."

"Fine."

"But if he gets killed . . ."

"I won't hold you responsible for his death."

"You won't have to," Clint said. "I would."

When Clint got to the livery Maxim was there, with not only his own horse saddled, but Duke as well. He was also sporting a bloody left hand.

"This gelding of yours is hell to saddle," he said. "He almost took my hand off."

"He doesn't like a lot of people."

"I can see that. So, did you talk to the judge?"

"I did."

"And?"

"You can come along."

"Great!"

"Just so long as you do what you're told."

Maxim frowned.

"I am the one with the badge, you know."

"I know," Clint said, "but I'm in charge."

Maxim shrugged and said, "Okay."

"So we're agreed on that?"

"Yes," Maxim said, "agreed."

"We'll need some supplies."

Maxim produced a burlap sack from the other side of his horse. It was hanging from his saddle horn.

"I thought of that. I also thought we should travel light, avoid having a packhorse to slow us down."

"That was good thinking."

Maxim almost preened at the compliment.

"Mount up, then," Clint said. "We're already starting an hour later than I'd intended."

As Maxim mounted Clint quickly checked his saddle, cinching it a bit tighter before mounting up, himself.

"This is gonna be great, Clint!" Maxim said enthusiastically. "I'll learn a lot."

"The first thing you've got to learn," Clint said, "is not to be so enthusiastic early in the morning."

"Got it."

"And to be quiet."

"Got it."

They'd ridden ten feet when Maxim asked, "Quiet for how long?"

NINE

Bass Reaves watched the smoke coming out of the tin pipe that was acting as a chimney for the little shack. Inside, he knew, were three men who would as soon kill him as look at him, but one of them was supposed to know where he could find Jim Webb.

All he had to do was wait for the great equalizer before moving in on them—nightfall.

In the shack were Doc Cryder, Mike Handy, and Dutch Cashman, all career criminals, all in their thirties, and all hungry for a big score and a woman.

"Not to mention a decent meal," Cashman said. He tossed his tin plate down on the table—but not before he had cleaned it. "I'm gettin' real tired of beans."

"It's not my fault we ran out of bacon," Handy said, stuffing his mouth with beans. When he was hungry he didn't care what he ate.

"I'm not talkin' about bacon," Cashman said. "I'm talking about a thick steak."

"Not much chance of that in the middle of the territories," Cryder said, "unless you can get some redskin to share some of his buffalo meat with you."

33

"Shows how much you know," Cashman said. "Buffalo's been gone for years."

"You know," Handy said, "you're always throwin' it in our faces how much smarter than us you are. Why don't you come up with a big score for us?"

"We'd have to leave the territories."

"We're all wanted everywhere else," Cryder pointed out. "Where can we go?"

"East," Cashman said, "west, north, south to Old Mexico. Pick a direction."

"We leave the territories we're gonna have lawmen on our asses."

"We got Judge Parker's badges after us now, anyway," Cashman said.

"Okay," Cryder said, "you pick a direction, Dutch, and I'll follow you."

Cashman looked at Handy.

"Mike?"

"Sure," Handy said, "why not? We ain't gettin' nothin' done just sittin' here."

"Where are we goin', Cash?" Cryder said.

Bass Reaves, who had been listening outside the door, kicked it in and said, "How about to hell?"

The men moved faster than he thought they would.

"No!" he shouted as they all kicked back their chairs, rose to their feet, and grabbed for their guns.

Reaves carried four guns, usually, because he always rode alone. He wore two revolvers with the butts forward, carried a Winchester and a double-barreled shotgun. He'd left the Winchester on his horse this time, and carried the shotgun. With three men going for their guns he triggered both barrels and hoped for the best. The sound was deafening in the small shack and the double-ought wreaked havoc as it tore through two of the three men who had been unfortunate enough to be standing too close together.

He dropped the shotgun and pulled both guns. The

third man, his movement for his own weapon arrested
by the sound of the shotgun, threw his hands in the air.

"Don't shoot," Dutch Cashman said.

On the floor Mike Handy rolled about, trying to hold
his insides in, while Cryder lay in a crumpled heap,
bloody and dead. Reaves knew by looking at Handy that
he'd be dead soon, as well.

He closed on Cashman and relieved him of his
weapon, tossing it into a corner.

"Who knows where Jim Webb is?" he demanded.

"W-what?" Cashman asked, confused.

"Which one of you knows where Webb is?" Reaves
shouted, louder this time. The fierce countenance of the
black man scared Cashman so much he shit his pants.
The smell, sharp and sickening, filled the room.

Reaves cocked the hammer on one of his six-guns.

"Last chance."

"Him, him!" Cashman said.

"Which one?"

"Handy."

"Which one?"

"The one rollin' around!"

Reaves brought the barrel of his uncocked gun up and
pistol-whipped Cashman into unconsciousness with one
blow.

After that he leaned over the dying man and rolled
him over. The man's face was gray and from experience
Reaves knew he was moments from death.

"Where's Jim Webb?" he demanded.

Mike Handy's eyes were clouding over and darkness
was crowding him from all sides. Still, he was able to
make out the face of the man looming over him.

"Come on!" Reaves shouted. "Where do I find Jim
Webb, damn it?"

Mike Handy's mouth moved, but he was speaking too
low for Reaves to hear him.

"What? What's that?" Reaves brought his ear down to the man's mouth.

"Go to hell, nigger," Mike Handy said and died, his death rattle in Bass Reaves's ear.

TEN

After four days of riding around the territories, Clint and Maxim thought they had a line on where Bass Reaves was. It appeared that Reaves was not traveling in a straight line. Apparently he was following up any whisper of where Jim Webb was, and for that reason he had been zigzagging his way back and forth across Indian Territory. Once he had even come close to Fort Smith, but then another whisper had taken him in the other direction.

"How are we gonna catch up to him this way?" Maxim asked, as they camped for their fourth night. "He could be anywhere."

"It's not as bad as it could be," Clint told him.

"It's not?"

"If he were chasing Webb in a straight line," Clint said, "he could be anywhere by now: California, Alaska, Mexico."

"Alaska," Maxim said. "I've never been to Alaska. Why don't we look there?"

"Finish your coffee. You've got the first watch."

In the morning Clint woke Maxim and handed him a cup of coffee.

37

"I think I figured it out last night," Maxim said. "Goin' in circles is better."

"You agree?"

"I do," Maxim said, "except for one thing."

"What's that?"

"Is he going in a widening circle," the younger man asked, "or a narrowing circle?"

"You're learning, Al," Clint said. "You're learning to ask the right questions."

"And what's the right answer?"

"I don't know."

Maxim sipped his coffee and looked up at Clint.

"You don't know the right answer?"

"No," Clint said, " 'I don't know' is the right answer."

Maxim scratched his head and said, "I reckon I'll have to think on that one awhile."

They broke camp and headed out, and by midafternoon they saw a small shack. There were no horses outside.

"Looks empty," Maxim said. "No horses."

"Look at the ground."

Maxim did.

"Tracks," Clint said.

"How old?"

"Days."

"So there was somebody here, but there ain't now," Maxim said.

"Assume that," Clint said, "and you might catch a bullet."

"So what do we do?"

"We approach," Clint said, "but with caution."

"Okay."

Maxim started his horse forward.

"On foot," Clint said.

Maxim reined in his horse said, "Okay," and dismounted, as did Clint. They left the horses where they were and approached on foot.

The stench hit them even before they reached the open door of the shack.

"Whew, what is that?" Maxim asked.

Clint knew what it was, but he decided to let Maxim see for himself. The younger man went into the shack, then came stumbling out, fell to his knees, and vomited in the dirt.

Clint steeled himself and went inside.

The men had been dead for days, and the heat had caused their bodies to bloat, and then burst. The bodies were covered with maggots. From the looks of them they'd been killed by blasts from a shotgun.

Suddenly, there was some small movement which Clint caught from the corner of his eye.

"We got one still alive in here," he called out. He didn't know if Maxim would bother to come back in, but he did.

"What?"

"Here," Clint said, moving to the other side of the shack.

The man had dragged himself into a corner. He didn't look injured, except for a welt above his left eye. His eyes were open but unfocused. The odor coming from him was one of human excrement, dried and old.

"What the hell—" Maxim said.

"Go to the horses and get some water," Clint said.

"Sure," Maxim said, glad to be sent from the shack.

"Take it easy, friend," Clint said.

At the sound of Clint's voice the man frowned. Suddenly, he was trying to focus his eyes.

"Who did this to you?" Clint asked.

The man's lips moved but nothing came out. They were parched and cracked. Maxim returned with a canteen. When Clint wet the man's lips, his tongue did not even come out to seek the moisture.

"I don't know if we're going to get anything out of him," Clint said. "He's pretty far gone."

"He ain't been shot," Maxim said.

"No, but he was whipped with a pistol."

"Why wasn't he shot, like the others?"

"I don't know." Clint looked at Maxim over his shoulder. "Does Reaves carry a shotgun?"

"He does," Maxim said. "Double-barreled. Also a Winchester and two six-guns."

"He might have done this, then."

"Looking for Webb?"

Clint nodded.

"See the door?"

Maxim looked and saw that it was hanging from one hinge.

"Kicked open," he said.

"Right. He must have surprised them and they went for their guns. He blasted those two, pistol-whipped this one."

"Why not kill him, too?"

"Maybe he didn't need to. Maybe this was the one who knew where Webb was."

"And if it was one of the other ones?"

"Then Reaves was out of luck." Clint looked at the man on the floor, whose eyes had become completely sightless. "Like this poor bastard."

ELEVEN

They buried the remains of the three dead men, although it took some persuading on Clint's part to get Maxim to touch them. Once they were all in the ground behind the shack, Clint checked the ground for sign.

"They had their horses back here. Somebody—maybe Reaves—must have scattered them."

"What about Reaves?"

"I see the tracks of three horses," Clint said, "but let's look around the shack."

They walked around and Clint found the tracks of a big man, with very large feet. He asked Maxim about Bass Reaves's feet.

"He's a big bastard," Maxim said, "so he's got real big feet. You can really hear him when he's walking down the street. His boots are heavy."

"So are these tracks," Clint said. "I mean, they were made by a big, heavy man."

"He ain't fat, though," Maxim said. "Reaves is a big man."

"Let's backtrack these boot prints."

They did so, walking their own horses behind them. Clint had been trying to educate Maxim on tracking ever since they left Fort Smith—not that he was a great tracker himself. He knew plenty of men who were better, but he could read sign well enough to track somebody like Bass Reaves—if these were, indeed, Reaves's tracks.

Finally, they found the place where the owner of the tracks had left his horse.

"Now what?" Maxim asked.

"Well, if we assume that it was Reaves who killed those men, then we have our first sign of him, and we have tracks to follow."

"And if it ain't him?"

Clint shrugged.

"Then we're following the wrong man."

"How are we gonna know for sure?"

"We'll know for sure," Clint said, "once we find whoever made these tracks. Come on, let's mount up. We've still got a few hours of daylight and I don't want to waste it."

"If we hadn't stopped to bury those maggot-infested bodies—"

"It doesn't matter who they were or what they did," Clint said sternly, "they deserved to be buried."

"Fine," Maxim said. "Whatever you say."

"That was the deal," Clint said, and nudged Duke in the sides to get him going.

When they camped for the night Maxim apologized for what he'd said about the dead men.

"I just—I ain't seen bodies in that condition before," he said. "How do they . . . blow up like that?"

"A doctor I know once told me that some kind of gas forms inside and expands as the temperature gets hotter. Eventually, the skin just bursts—"

"Okay," Maxim said, "never mind." He swallowed hard and dumped the remains of his coffee on the fire.

"Tell me something," he said, changing the subject.

"What?"

"Why's the judge want Reaves tracked?"

"He never told you?"

"He never asked me to do it," Maxim said, "just some of the others. See, I ain't been a deputy that long."

"He's worried about him."

"About Reaves?"

Clint nodded.

"Why?"

"The judge just doesn't think he's himself lately," Clint said. "He wants him stopped before he does something he'll be sorry for."

"Like what?"

"I don't know," Clint said. "Maybe killing the wrong man."

"Long as I've known Bass Reaves—and it ain't all that long—he ain't never killed the wrong man."

"Well," Clint said, "there's always a first time. I'll take the first watch tonight. I'm not sleepy."

"Well, I sure am," Maxim said.

"I'll wake you in four hours."

Maxim rolled himself up in his blanket and was asleep in minutes. Clint made a fresh pot of coffee and laid his rifle down beside him. Nobody was hunting them, but in the territories it was good to stay alert. Not only were there Indians to worry about, but Comancheros and all shapes and sizes of predators—two-legged and four.

Clint thought a bit about Bass Reaves and what he was doing. Basically, he was supposed to be a delivery boy. Come home, Bass, all is forgiven; but the more dead bodies they came across, the harder it was going to be to simply deliver a message. Whatever the three men in the shack had done, they had not deserved to die so horribly—particularly the third one, who had died so slowly.

Clint hoped that it wasn't Bass Reaves who had killed them, and that this wasn't the black marshal's trail they were following, but his instincts told him that he had, and it was.

TWELVE

Bass Reaves rode into the town of Culver Flats with one thing on his mind—Jim Webb. Of course, he was also thinking of a bath and a meal and a room for the night. But his primary concern was—and had been for weeks—finding some trace of Jim Webb.

Webb was a hard man to track because, just as Bass Reaves had his contacts in the territories, so did Jim Webb. Reaves and Webb were equally at home in this part of the country, and that made this particular cat-and-mouse game one that would probably go on for a long time.

Reaves didn't care how long it took, however. He was going to find Jim Webb and administer swift justice. He'd save Judge Parker the bother of a hanging, even if the judge wouldn't thank him for it.

Reaves had a history of bringing men back dead. Most people thought he did it that way because it was easier. He knew that he did it that way when they gave him no other choice.

This time, however, with Jim Webb, the choice was going to be his own.

Webb was coming back to Fort Smith tied over his saddle.

45

• • •

The only bathtubs in town were at the barbershop, and the owner wasn't happy about letting a black man use one.

"Marshal," he said, out of deference to Reaves's badge, but with no respect for the man wearing it, "I can't let you use one of my tubs. I only got two, and if the men in town found out you used one—"

Reaves pushed three times the amount of money the barber was charging for the tubs into the man's hand and said, "Make sure nobody finds out, then."

"What?"

"Don't let anyone in while I'm taking a bath."

"But—"

"I don't take that long."

"But—" the man said, only Reaves was gone.

The barber put the money away and made a face. He was going to have to find out which tub the nigger used and then put boiling water in it. He only hoped nobody found out about it.

Maybe there was another way.

Bass Reaves never allowed himself the luxury of a hot bath. A man could relax himself to death in hot water. He used tepid water, and never soaked. He got in, washed himself, and got out.

That's what saved his life.

The men who kicked in the door ten minutes after he got into the bath expected to find him still in the tub. Instead, Bass was standing up, drying himself off with a towel when they came charging in. They had their guns in their hands and began firing at the empty tub. They made several holes in it before they realized it was empty. For a moment there was only the sound of the water leaking from the holes in the tub onto the floor and then both men heard the sound of both hammers being cocked on a shotgun.

• • •

The barber heard the sounds of the shots, and then the twin barrels of a shotgun going off almost as one. He hoped that in killing the nigger there was no damage done to his tubs. He hurried back to have a look.

As the barber came rushing into the room, Bass grabbed him from behind, his huge forearm going across the man's throat, constricting his breathing.

"Who told you to send those men?" Bass demanded. "Was it Webb?"

"W-who?" the barber rasped.

"Jim Webb! Did he tell you to send those men after me?" Bass demanded.

"I—can't—talk!"

Reaves released his hold on the man just enough to let him breathe and talk.

"Now tell me about Webb."

"I don't know any Webb," the barber said.

"Then why did you send those men to kill me?" Reaves demanded.

"I didn't want you using my tub."

At that moment the man became aware of the water on the floor, and saw the holes in his tub.

"Oh, no!" he wailed.

Then he saw the mangled mess Reaves's shotgun had made of the two men he'd paid to kill the black man.

"Oh, Jesus!"

Reaves released the barber, turned him around, and gave him a shove that sent him backpedaling toward the tub. He banged into it and then fell in. There was enough water left to soak him.

Bass put down the empty shotgun and took his pistol from his holster. He walked to the tub and pointed the gun at the frightened barber.

"Nobody kills for a bathtub," he said, cocking the hammer back. "Now, you're going to tell me the truth, or die for trying to have a federal marshal killed."

"No, wait—"

"Put that gun up, mister."

Reaves froze, but kept his gun pointed at the wet barber.

"This ain't none of your concern, mister," Reaves said, hoping that whoever was behind him wasn't another hired gun.

"I'm afraid it is, friend," the unseen man said. "See, I'm the sheriff around here, and I got my gun pointed at the back of your head. I understand you people have hard heads. Do we want to test that out?"

"I got a badge of my own," Reaves said.

There was a pause, and then the man said, "Where?"

"It's on my shirt," Reaves said. He was wearing nothing but his underwear at the moment.

The sheriff looked around and saw the shirt on a chair.

"Just stand easy and I'll take a look."

Reaves kept his gun pointed at the barber, whose eyes were still wide.

The sheriff walked over, picked Reaves's shirt up off the chair, and looked at the front of it. He saw the badge pinned to it.

"One of Judge Parker's?" he asked.

"That's right."

The sheriff came right up next to Reaves and holstered his own gun. They looked at the barber together.

"What'd he do?" he asked.

"Hired those two to kill me."

Reaves jerked his head at the two mangled bodies lying in the corner. As much as the shotgun blast had torn up their bodies, their faces were virtually untouched.

"I don't know them," the man said. "Must have just ridden in today."

"One of them's got a fresh haircut," Bass said. "You can still smell the lilac water on him."

The sheriff sniffed.

"Yeah, you can." He looked down at the barber. "You hire them two to kill this man, Harlan?"

"Well . . ."

"You better tell me the truth, Harlan."

"Well . . . I couldn't let him use my tub! Sheriff, he's a nigger!"

"He's a federal marshal working out of Judge Parker's court, Harlan," the local lawman said, "and you tried to have him killed. If he took you back to Fort Smith the judge would hang you."

"You ain't gonna let him take me there, are you, Sheriff?"

"No, Harlan," the sheriff said, "I'm not." He looked at Bass Reaves. "Go ahead and shoot him if you want to. You got a right."

THIRTEEN

Clint and Maxim rode into Culver Flats three days after Bass Reaves had taken his bath.

"You sure them tracks led here?" Maxim asked.

"Right here."

"It's so small," Maxim said. "Why would Bass stop here?"

"Maybe to eat, or sleep," Clint said. "Who knows? Maybe he thought Webb was here."

"How long we gonna stay?"

"That depends."

"On what?"

"On whether or not he's still here," Clint said.

"Bass?"

Clint nodded.

"Or whoever's tracks we've been following," he said.

"And how do we find out?"

"We talk to the local law first," Clint said.

They found the sheriff's office and dismounted in front of it.

"Ain't you gonna tie your horse?" Maxim asked, as he tied his own to a hitching post.

"He's not going to go anywhere."

51

They mounted the boardwalk together, knocked on the door, and went inside.

The man behind the desk wore the sheriff's badge and stood as they entered, eyeing them warily. Clint had a feeling the man was good at his job. He wore his gun, even in his office, and he looked ready and able to use it.

Clint could see the man's shoulders relax a bit when his eyes fell on the badge that Maxim was wearing.

"Sheriff," Clint said, "I'm Clint Adams, and this is Marshal Maxim."

"One of Judge Parker's boys," the sheriff said.

"That's right," Maxim said.

"He's signing them up young these days," the local lawman said. "My name's Sheriff Ralph Gar."

"Sheriff Gar." Both Clint and Maxim shook the man's hand.

"Why don't you fellas have a chair?"

They both sat, and only then did the sheriff sit, as well.

"I guess you're here about your colleague."

"Colleague?" Maxim asked.

"The black marshal," Gar said. "What's his name? Bass Reaves?"

"That's him," Maxim said.

"He was here?"

"Three days ago." Gar leaned forward. "He is a marshal, isn't he? I mean, I considered for a minute he might have stolen the badge."

"No," Maxim said, "he's a marshal, all right."

Gar nodded his satisfaction at not having been bamboozled and sat back.

"How long was he here?" Clint asked.

"Just a day," Gar said. "Long enough to kill two men and nearly kill a third."

"Who did he kill?" Maxim asked.

"A couple of drifters," Gar said. "Nobody's gonna miss them."

"What happened?" Clint asked. "Who's the man he almost killed?"

"The barber."

"The barber?" It sounded to Clint like Reaves had finally snapped.

"Apparently, the barber—whose name is Harlan Taylor—hired the two men to rough up your marshal before he could use one of his bathtubs."

"They were gonna kill him over a bathtub?"

"Letting a black man use his bathtub would have ruined it . . . he says," the sheriff replied. "It made sense to him. Besides, I don't think he wanted them to kill Reaves, but that seemed to be their solution to the problem."

"But he killed them."

"Blew them in half with a shotgun."

Clint kept himself from looking at Maxim, although he knew the young marshal was looking at him. This left no doubt in their minds that Reaves had killed the men in the shack.

"And the barber?"

"Well, I got there just in time to keep Reaves from making a big mistake," Gar said. "The barber wasn't even armed."

"And you think Reaves was going to kill him?" Clint asked.

"He seemed mad enough."

"Well, I guess so," Maxim said indignantly. "Killing a man over a bathtub?"

"Well, he didn't kill the barber, although he seemed to think that Jim Webb had put Taylor up to hiring those two men."

"You know Webb?" Clint asked.

"Sure, who doesn't, around here?" Gar said. "I mean, I know of him."

"What happened after that?"

"Well, Reaves decided to leave town once he was convinced that Jim Webb had nothing to do with what happened," Gar said.

"And did he use the tub?" Maxim asked.

"Oh, yeah," Gar said. "He got his bath, all right."

"Good," Maxim said. "I hope the barber had to throw it out."

"He patched it up," Gar said. "In fact, I think he's still got boiling water in it."

FOURTEEN

"You let him go?" Maxim asked unnecessarily.

"It was self-defense," Gar said. "Besides, he was a marshal, and all he did was scare poor Taylor half to death. Also, he was one big, mean-looking hombre. You bet I let him go. I wanted him out of this town as soon as possible."

Clint couldn't blame the man for that. It sounded like there had been a lot of commotion in the one afternoon Reaves had been in town. He'd been in that situation himself, when somebody decided he wanted to make a name for himself. Since Clint was usually the one left standing, he was usually the one the local law asked to please leave town.

"Did you happen to hear him say where he was going?" Maxim asked.

"I don't think he knew where he was going," Gar said, rubbing his jaw. "He's still on the trail of Jim Webb, I guess."

"It's more of a sure bet than a guess, Sheriff," Clint said.

"What's he got against Webb, other than that he's wanted?"

"I guess we'll find that out when we catch up to him," Clint said.

"You boys are huntin' him? For the judge?"

Clint stood up, and Maxim followed.

"Just to deliver a message," Clint said. "Thanks for your help, Sheriff."

"You plan on staying in town?"

"Just for the night," Clint said. "We'll be leaving in the morning."

"Good," Gar said, then added, "no offense."

"None taken, Sheriff," Clint said.

"It's just that—well, you bein' who you are and all, and the marshal here sportin' that badge, and we already had all that trouble with Bass Reaves—"

"No explanation necessary, Sheriff," Clint said. "We'll be on our way. We just need a meal, a beer, and a bed, and come morning we're gone."

"They make a good steak over at the hotel," Gar said. "Cold beer, too."

Clint wondered if that was true, or if the sheriff just wanted to keep them out of the saloons, where someone might recognize Clint or decide that Maxim's badge would be a good target.

"Thanks again for your help, Sheriff," Clint said, and he and Maxim left the office.

"Sounds like he did right by Bass," Maxim said, "but was he tryin' to keep us out of the saloons?"

"That's what it sounded like," Clint said. "Can't say I blame him. It would sure make his job easier if we stayed out of sight."

"Hidin', you mean," Maxim said, with a young man's bravado.

"Let's take the horses to the livery," Clint said. "We can talk about that after we eat."

They walked their horses to the livery, then carried their saddlebags and rifles to the hotel with them. They each got a room, took their things up, and then came back down to the dining room.

Clint's steak was bloody, the way he liked it, and he grimaced as he watched Maxim cut into his well-done meat.

"How can you eat that?" he asked. "The flavor's been burned out of it."

"This is the way I like it," Maxim said. "Can't stand red meat."

The vegetables were steamed to perfection, and the beer—as promised—was cold. This took care of any reason they might have had for leaving the hotel, except for two: gambling or a woman.

Over coffee Maxim said, "Now, let's talk about this business of hidin' inside."

"It's got nothing to do with hiding, Al," Clint said. "The sheriff is just trying to avoid trouble. Besides, we're only going to be here for one night."

"That's right," Maxim said, "which means it'll be my only chance to get a woman for a while."

"You need a woman that bad?"

"Sure, don't you?"

Clint smirked and said, "Well, you're younger than I am."

"You ain't that old," Maxim said. "Come on, there's got to be a cathouse in town somewhere."

"Not for me," Clint said.

Maxim frowned.

"You really don't like women?"

"I love women," Clint said—and he thought the younger man looked relieved—"but I don't like paying for them."

"Takes too long the other way," Maxim said, "and I don't have that much time, remember?"

"I'll tell you what," Clint said. "We'll find out from the waiter if there's a whorehouse in town. If there is, you can go there, but nowhere else. Is that a deal?"

"It's a deal."

"You won't go to a saloon?"

"Not if there's a cathouse," Maxim said. "That should take care of my needs very nicely."

FIFTEEN

There was, indeed, a whorehouse in town, and the waiter was only too glad to give Maxim detailed directions of how to get to it.

"Ask for Elaine," the waiter said. "She's the best girl there."

Maxim looked the man up and down and decided he was fiftyish and portly, and probably had a different idea of what a whorehouse's "best" girl was, but he thanked him, anyway.

"Sure you don't want to come?" Maxim asked Clint as they left the hotel.

"I'll walk there with you," Clint said, "if only to keep you out of trouble."

"Now, what call do you have to think that I'd get in trouble?" Maxim asked good-naturedly. "You don't know me that well."

"You're young," Clint said. "That gives me cause enough."

The whorehouse was at the far end of town, which, Clint thought, figured. They had to walk the length of the town without encountering some drunk with a quick gun hand. Still, it was a small town, and since it had already

59

had its fair share of trouble for the week maybe their chances were good.

But he wouldn't bet on it.

Dirk Fletcher, Zeke Masters, and Cort Sherman had heard the stories about Marshal Bass Reaves being in town. They had arrived the day after he left.

"We could have taken him," Fletcher had said, when they heard. "Bass Reaves, one of Judge Parker's marshals, and we could have taken him."

"The nigger marshal?" Masters had asked.

"That's right."

"He's got a rep," Sherman had replied.

"I know it," Fletcher said, "but we could have taken him."

Fletcher had spent all that day and the next pissing and moaning about how they had missed an opportunity to take Bass Reaves. By the time Clint and Maxim arrived in town, Fletcher had his partners convinced.

It was sheer coincidence that Zeke Masters picked the same night to go to the whorehouse that Al Maxim was there.

Clint walked Maxim to the house and watched him walk in. Zeke Masters walked past Maxim as he was going out, and his eyes lit up when he saw the deputy marshal's badge on his chest. If they could have taken one marshal, he thought, why not another?

He ran to tell his partners what he saw. He didn't recognize Clint, and since he wasn't wearing a badge, the man didn't pay him any mind at all.

Clint turned and walked back to the hotel. Masters went in the other direction, to a rooming house he and his friends were staying in.

"Are you sure?" Dirk Fletcher asked Masters.

"I know a badge when I see one, Dirk."

"But a deputy marshal's badge?"

"It said it right on it."

"What are the chances," Sherman asked, "of two marshals being in this town in one week?"

"But who was this one?" Fletcher asked. "At least Bass Reaves I heard of. What did this one look like?"

"Young," Masters said, "real young."

"And was he with anyone?"

"Another man."

"Also a marshal?"

"No," Masters said, "he wasn't wearing no badge."

"Then who was he?"

"I don't know."

"Well, if the marshal is with somebody we got to find out who he is before we do anything," Fletcher said. "I haven't lived to a ripe old age going off half-cocked."

Dirk Fletcher was all of thirty-two. His companions were also in their early thirties.

"So what do we do?" Masters asked.

"We find out where they're staying, and we find out who they are."

"How do we do that?" Sherman asked.

"Cort," Fletcher asked, "how about a whore?"

"Well, I—"

"On me."

"Well," Sherman said, licking his lips, "if you're payin'."

SIXTEEN

Al Maxim had picked out a girl who looked about nineteen, but was probably closer to twenty-five—his own age. She was dressed young, and probably passed for fifteen up to a couple of years ago. He didn't care, though. He just needed a woman, and she was the one he picked.

They went up to her room where she undressed herself, and then him, talking to him the whole time. When she had him naked and his penis was stiff, standing straight out from his pubic hair, she got down on her knees and began to coo to it, holding it in both hands, fondling it, stroking it until he thought he'd burst.

"Come on, girl!" he said anxiously. "Get on the bed."

"But I want to kiss it, and taste it—"

"You can do that later," he said. "Right now I just wanna be in you."

He reached down and lifted her, his hands on her elbows. She was slender, with small, pale breasts that had pink nipples. He pushed her down on the bed, and she giggled as he crawled atop her and began poking at her with his penis. She wasn't wet so she reached down between her legs and took hold of him. She held him

63

against her while he pushed, and eventually he poked right into her.

From that point on Al Maxim was delirious and happy as he slammed into the girl over and over again, and he didn't even notice the bored look on her face as she stared up at the ceiling and thought about her bank account. She'd been doing this for six years now, and she almost had enough money to leave town.

Suddenly, she realized he had finished and rolled off of her.

"That was great," she said.

"It sure was," he replied, breathing heavily. "Just gimme a few minutes and I can get hard again. Then you can taste it, like you wanted to."

"Honey," she said, "you already had me. If you want to do anything else it's gonna cost extra."

"What?"

"Of course," she said coyly, "we don't have to tell anybody else that we did it again." She stroked his flaccid penis, wondering if he really would be able to get hard again. He was young enough, but he sure was in a hurry. "We can just settle it between ourselves. I won't charge you as much as the house would."

She slid her hand down to his testicles and then touched a spot just below them that made him jump. She went back to stroking his penis, which was beginning to stretch itself out again. Yeah, he'd be able to do it again—probably no better than before, but at least she'd be able to charge him extra.

"How much would it be?" he asked breathlessly. "I mean, to go again."

She slid down between his legs and nuzzled his stiffening penis with her nose, flicked at it with the tip of her tongue.

"We can talk about that," she said, "later."

She took him into her mouth, causing him to catch his breath, and began to suck him avidly.

• • •

When Al Maxim came back downstairs the madam asked, "How did you like Rosemary?"

"I liked her just fine."

"You were up there a long time."

"Well . . . it sometimes takes me a while."

"Yeah," the heavyset woman said, "and sometimes my girls like to make their own deals."

The madam was in her fifties, with flaccid skin under her chin and her upper arms that wiggled when she talked or laughed. She was doing both now, and her loose skin was flapping around like a flag in a breeze.

"I wouldn't know—"

"Forget it, Marshal," she said. "It ain't your problem, it's mine. Just tell your friends you had a good time here."

"I will," he said, even though he knew he only had one friend in town and Clint wouldn't be caught dead in a whorehouse. "I sure will."

As Maxim left, a disconsolate Cort Sherman left right behind him, following him. Fletcher had teased him about having a whore. He'd had to stay downstairs in the sitting room with the girls, getting teased, drinking whiskey, and waiting for the deputy to come back down. In the end he never even got his hand on a bare breast before he had to leave to follow the deputy.

He tailed Maxim back to the hotel where he and Clint were staying, and waited just outside the lobby, where he could see in. When the marshal went upstairs he entered the lobby and approached the front desk. He took out a dollar, showed it to the clerk, and left with not only the marshal's name but the name of the man who had checked in with him.

He wasn't sure that Fletcher was going to like what he'd found out.

SEVENTEEN

"Say that name again," Dirk Fletcher told Cort Sherman. "Slowly."

"Clint . . . Adams," Sherman repeated.

"The Clint Adams?" Fletcher asked.

"I don't know how many there are, Dirk."

"We're talking about the Gunsmith?" Dirk Fletcher said, laughing.

"What's so funny, Dirk?" Masters asked.

"Don't you see?" Fletcher asked. "This is even better than Bass Reaves."

"Yeah, but the Gunsmith has a bigger rep," Masters said.

"That's what I mean."

"But . . . he's fast!" Cort Sherman said.

"He used to be fast," Dirk Fletcher said. "He's been around forever. Don't you see? He's *old*!"

"He didn't look that old to me," Masters said.

"You said yourself you didn't take a good look at him when you saw he wasn't wearing a badge."

"So you want to go after the Gunsmith?" Zeke Masters asked.

"Well, sure," Fletcher said. "The three of us can take him."

67

Zeke Masters and Cort Sherman exchanged a glance. Fletcher walked up to them and put a hand on each of their shoulders.

"Come on, Zeke," he said, "you're *fast*. And, Cort, you always hit what you aim at."

"But . . . you're better than either one of us with a gun, Dirk."

"I know," Fletcher said, squeezing their shoulders so hard they both flinched, "that's what I'm talking about. The three of us can take him."

"And what about the marshal?" Masters asked.

"We'll take care of him first," Fletcher said, "and then we'll go after the jackpot."

Cort Sherman frowned.

"What jackpot?"

"Clint Adams," Fletcher said, releasing their shoulders and walking to the window to look outside. "He's walking around out there and he's our jackpot."

The two men exchanged another look behind Fletcher's back. They still weren't convinced, but they both knew they'd go along with Fletcher, convinced or not.

That was the nature of their relationship with him. He led, and they followed.

EIGHTEEN

When Maxim returned to the hotel he knocked on Clint's door. When Clint opened it the young deputy smiled and said, "I'm back, safe and sound."

"You look satisfied, too."

"I am," Maxim said. "The girl I picked was very enthusiastic about her work."

Sure, Clint thought, you were paying her to be enthusiastic.

"What've you been doin'?"

"Just sitting in here reading a Mark Twain novel."

"Reading?" Maxim looked as if he didn't understand the concept of reading a book. Wanted posters, maybe, or letters, or even the labels on whiskey bottles, but a book?

"Sounds excitin'," he said.

"It's not," Clint said, "but then, it's not supposed to be."

"How about we go and get a drink?"

"I don't think—"

"One beer," Maxim said. "Come on, I'll buy."

"On what you make as a deputy?"

Maxim made a face.

"You're right," he said, "and there won't be much

69

money waiting for me when I get back from this trip, because there's no price on Bass's head.''

"That's right."

"I wonder if any of those fellers he's killed had prices on their heads."

"It doesn't matter if they do or not," Clint said, "we're going forward, not back."

"Okay, then I guess you'll have to buy me a drink," Maxim said. "One beer . . . just one . . . come on . . . whataya say?"

"Are you going to pester me about this?"

Maxim nodded.

"All night."

Clint sighed.

"Then I guess I'm better off giving in now, huh?"

"Definitely."

"Okay." Clint left the door open and retrieved his gun belt and his hat. "One beer, right?"

"Right."

"And then we come right back here and turn in. I want to get an early start in the morning."

"Right back here," Maxim agreed.

Clint closed his door, and they left and headed for the saloon.

When they entered Clint saw Sheriff Gar standing at the bar. He tugged on Maxim's sleeve and led the way to where the sheriff was standing.

"Sheriff," Clint said.

"Mr. Adams," the sheriff said, "Deputy. I thought you were going to stay at your hotel."

"We thought we'd stop for one beer before we turned in," Clint said. "And how much safer could we be than to have it with you?"

"You followed me here?"

"No," Clint said, "we just happened to run into you. Making your rounds?"

"I am."

There was no drink in front of the man, so Clint assumed he'd arrived just moments before them.

"Why not let us buy you a beer?"

Gar considered it for a moment, then said, "Sure, why not? Henry? Three beers. This gentleman is paying."

The bartender brought over the three beers and Clint paid him right away. The three men picked them up and sipped them down to various levels. Actually, Maxim gulped half of his while Clint and the sheriff both took a couple of sips.

"Doesn't look like a very exciting place," Maxim said to Gar, looking around the saloon.

About three quarters of the tables were occupied, but there wasn't one poker game in session. Also, there were two girls working the floor, but they were rather tired-looking. Maxim thought that all the girls at the whorehouse had looked better. Thinking about his time with Rosemary made him start to get hard again, so he tried to distract himself with conversation.

"It's not an exciting place," Gar said.

"Are we talking about the saloon," Maxim asked, "or the town?"

"Both," Gar said. "It's a quiet town most of the time. We don't get a lot of strangers stopping here. This week is an exception. There was your partner, Reaves, then three other men, and now you."

"Three other men?" Clint asked.

"Drifters," Gar said, "and if you're wonderin', Jim Webb ain't one of them."

"Has Jim Webb ever been here?"

"Not that I know of."

Clint decided that Bass Reaves had simply stopped in this town for a bath, and probably for a meal and a night in a real bed. Maybe he hadn't expected all that commotion over a bath. Whatever had happened, he didn't think that Reaves was following any lead to Webb when he rode in.

He sipped some more of his beer, noticing that Maxim was lowering the level of his at a faster pace. Abruptly, the sheriff drained his and slapped the empty mug down on the bar.

"Another?" Clint asked.

"No," Gar said, "and I'd buy you one, but I have to go back on my rounds."

"That's okay," Clint said. "We only stopped in for the one."

"Well, good night, then," Gar said, "and good-bye, since you'll be leaving at first light."

"That we will," Clint said. "Thanks for you help."

"Thanks for the drink."

Sheriff Gar walked out and Clint swirled the beer in his mug, then looked at Maxim, who had about a mouthful left.

"I ain't done," Maxim said.

"I can see that."

Maxim looked around.

"You'd think there would at least be a poker game going."

"Yeah," Clint said, "you would think so." He finished his beer and put his mug down on the bar.

"Another?" the bartender asked, appearing immediately to do his job.

"No thanks," Clint said. He turned and looked at Maxim, who still had the same mouthful of beer at the bottom of his mug.

"That's going to get warm," he said.

"We could cool it off—"

"Al."

"But can't we—"

"We agreed," Clint said. "One beer."

"I know, but—"

"Never mind."

Clint was about to say more when the doors opened and admitted three men, all wearing trail clothes, all wearing their guns tied down.

These, Clint assumed, were the other three strangers in town, and they didn't look too friendly.

NINETEEN

"I knew we should have stayed at the hotel," Clint said.

"What?" Maxim asked. "Why?" His eyes followed Clint's and he saw the three men. "You know those three men?"

"No," Clint said, "but I know the type. They're on the prod. We've got to avoid them."

"Why should that worry you?" Maxim asked. "You're Clint Adams."

"That's why it worries me."

"I don't understand."

"You wouldn't."

"Why not? Because I'm young? I know one thing for sure," Maxim said.

"And what's that?"

"I wish I had a rep like yours. I'm *gonna* get a rep like yours."

"And how are you going to do that, Al?"

Maxim finished his beer and put the empty mug down on the bar.

"Maybe by not avoiding hard cases like those three."

The three men walked to the bar and ordered beer. Before Clint could stop Maxim he marched over to them.

"You gents got a problem?"

Dirk Fletcher looked at his partners, then at the young deputy.

"Deputy," he said, "now, why would you think we have a problem?"

"Seems you were looking at me when you came in."

"Was I?" Fletcher asked. "Well, maybe that's because you're such a handsome young feller, with that shiny badge and all. Is that shiny badge really yours? Or did you take it off your daddy's shirt?"

Masters and Sherman laughed along with Fletcher at his joke.

"Oh, it's mine, all right," Maxim said. "Given to me all legal like by Judge Parker."

"Judge Parker gave that badge to a youngster like you?" Fletcher asked. He looked at his friends. "You know, I heard there was another deputy in town a few days ago, a nigger. Boys, seems like the judge is gettin' desperate for men. He's hirin' niggers and kids. Maybe we should go to Fort Smith and get some deputy badges of our own."

"Maybe we should," Sherman said, chuckling.

Clint knew when the three men walked in that they'd be trouble, but he hadn't expected Maxim to walk right into it and make the problem worse.

"Al," he said, coming up behind Maxim, "I think we'd better go."

Fletcher looked at Clint and asked Maxim, "Who's this? Your daddy?"

"No, he ain't my daddy," Maxim said. "Don't worry about him, you're talkin' to me."

"But he's talkin' to you," Fletcher said.

"Al—" He touched the deputy's arm.

"Leave me be, Clint!" Maxim snapped, jerking his arm away.

"Clint?" Fletcher asked. "Would that be Clint Adams?"

"That's right."

"Well, boys," Fletcher said to his friends while looking at Clint, "we better back off, here. The little deputy's got a big friend."

"You don't gotta worry about him," Maxim said. "This is between you and me."

"What's between you and them, Al?" Clint asked. "They haven't done anything."

"That's right, Little Deputy," Fletcher said. "Listen to your big friend. We ain't done nothin'."

"You ain't showin' this badge no respect, that's what you're doin'."

"No," Fletcher said, "that's what we *ain't* doin'." Suddenly, Fletcher's amiable look gave way to a hard one. "Now run along, Little Deputy. Me and my friends just came in for a drink."

"Don't call me that."

"What?" Fletcher asked. "Little Deputy?"

"That's right."

"Or what?"

"Al—"

"Or I'll make you sorry."

"And how will you do that . . . Little Deputy?"

"Why, you—"

Maxim went for his gun, but Clint was ready for him. He jammed his hand down on the deputy's so he couldn't get his gun out and then hit him over the head with the butt of his own gun. He caught the younger man as he slumped and lifted him over his shoulder, holstering his gun. Then he looked at Fletcher and the two other men.

"Forget about him," he said to them. "He had a little too much to drink."

"Well, now, Mr. Gunsmith, he said some pretty insultin' things to us," Fletcher said. "I don't know as we can forget them so easily."

"Seems to me there were things said on both sides,"

Clint said. "I think you should all just forget it."

Fletcher turned his body to face Clint, as did the two men behind him.

"Are you tellin' us what to do, Mr. Gunsmith?"

"That's right, friend," Clint said, "I'm telling you what to do."

Clint didn't wait for a reply. He walked out of the saloon, carrying Al Maxim like he was a sack of potatoes.

TWENTY

Maxim didn't come to until Clint dumped him on the bed in his hotel room.

"What the—you hit me!" he exclaimed, holding his head.

"I did it to keep you from making a mistake," Clint said. "What were you trying to prove, picking a fight with three men?"

"I was just picking a fight with the one who was doing the talking."

"I told you I've known those kind of men," Clint said. "He never would have faced you alone. You would have had to face all three."

"Well," Maxim said, swinging his legs around and planting his feet on the floor, "you were there to back me up."

"What makes you think I would have?" Clint asked.

"Well . . . wouldn't you have?"

"Maybe," Clint said, "if you had asked me first— but I don't back every bonehead play I see. Next time don't go picking a fight without checking with me first. I'm supposed to be in charge, remember our agreement?"

"I remember," Maxim said. "Oh, my head hurts. Did you have to hit me so hard?"

"I always hit hard," Clint said, "when I'm dealing with a hard head."

"Yeah, yeah . . ."

In the saloon Fletcher, Masters, and Sherman found themselves a table.

"That was close," Masters said. "I thought we were gonna have to face both of them."

"I thought we might find the deputy alone," Fletcher said.

"Why'd Adams drag him off like that?" Sherman asked. "Was he afraid?"

"I told you," Fletcher said, "he's gettin' old, losin' his nerve. This ain't even gonna be as hard as I thought it might."

"You thought it was gonna be *hard*?" Masters asked.

"Well, not so hard, but not easy, either," Fletcher said.

"We still gonna take the deputy first?" Sherman asked.

"That's the way I want to do it," Fletcher said, "but we'll have to find him alone."

"What if they leave town tomorrow?" Masters asked. "What if they're only here for one day?"

"We still have tonight," Fletcher said, "and tomorrow morning to think of something."

"Thinking of something," Sherman said, "that's your department."

"Yeah," Masters said. "We'll just sit around and wait until you do."

"Well, sitting around is something you boys do very well."

Masters and Sherman exchanged a glance, both unsure about whether or not they had just been insulted.

•   •   •

"So now you see what can happen when you go out for one beer," Clint said to Maxim, who was still holding his head.

"I've got a lump," Maxim complained, probing with his fingers.

"Let me see."

Clint did some probing himself, causing Maxim to cry out in pain.

"I didn't break the skin," he said. "You'll be all right in the morning."

"I better be," Maxim said. "I ain't lookin' forward to riding all morning with a headache."

"Well, get some sleep and I'll come and get you in the morning," Clint said.

"I just hope you don't find me dead in bed," Maxim said.

"I didn't hit you *that* hard, Al."

"Didn't have to hit me at all," the deputy muttered.

"Good night, Al," Clint said, and left the room.

TWENTY-ONE

"They're leavin' in the morning," Fletcher said, as he entered the room Sherman and Masters were sharing.

Sherman, who had been asleep, rubbed his eyes and asked, "How do you know?"

"I asked around, that's how I know," Fletcher said. "The desk clerk at their hotel talked to me for a few dollars, said he was to have their bill ready this morning. Also, the liveryman is supposed to have their horses and supplies ready at first light."

"That means they'll be leavin' the hotel together in the mornin'," Masters said, "We don't want to take them together."

"No, we don't," Fletcher said.

"So what do we do?" Sherman asked.

"Right now we get some sleep," Fletcher said. "I'll think of something during the night."

"I *was* asleep," Sherman complained.

"Well, go back to sleep," Fletcher said. "I'll wake you both up early. Whatever we're gonna do, we'll have to get to it before they can leave."

"When are they supposed to leave?" Masters asked.

"First light."

"*First* light?" Sherman complained. "That's early!"

"Well, then, get to sleep," Fletcher said, heading for the door. "What are you talkin' to me for?"

Fletcher stormed out of the room, and the two men looked at each other before rolling over in their beds and trying to get back to sleep.

Fletcher went to his room, pulled off his boots, hung his gun belt on the bedpost, and lay down on the bed fully dressed. He had to come up with a plan by morning, a plan that would not allow Clint Adams to get away. His first idea had been to kill one of Judge Parker's men, but now he knew that this deputy was just a kid. Clint Adams, the Gunsmith, was now the primary target. He wasn't all that sure that the three of them could take Adams, but they certainly wouldn't be able to take Adams and the deputy, no matter how young and inexperienced the other man was. They were still going to have to separate the two of them.

He just had to come up with a safe way to do it.

Similarly, Clint was lying in his bed, also trying to come up with a plan of action. Bass Reaves's trail had led here, and he had, indeed, been here and caused a commotion—his fault or not. They now knew that the trail they had been following was his. All that remained now was to try to pick up the trail once again outside of town. There were so many horses up and down the streets and in and out of the livery that picking it up in town again would be hopeless—and finding it again outside of town was no guarantee, either. For some men, maybe, but while Clint could read sign, he was no expert tracker.

There were also the three hard cases to worry about. Were they going to go away, or would he and Maxim have to deal with them before they left town? And in a firefight, how reliable was Maxim going to be?

Clint was afraid there was only one way to find that out, for sure.

• • •

In the town of Selma, some forty miles away from Culver Flats, Bass Reaves was still totally unaware of what was going on behind him. He was, however, curious that he had not heard from Judge Parker in some time. It wasn't like the judge to give up that way. He'd expected to find telegrams from Parker waiting for him in every town in the territories, urging him to return to Fort Smith.

Bass Reaves respected no man he had ever met the way he respected Judge Isaac Parker. It was because of the judge that he had grown up to be somebody, which was not something every black boy Reaves's age thought about.

It was more than likely that Parker was sending someone after him. Reaves didn't think any of his fellow deputies would take on the assignment, so the judge was probably going to call on someone else. That meant there was a good chance Reaves might run into some stranger who was looking for him, carrying a message from Judge Parker—but Reaves was carrying a hair trigger around with him these days, which was why he had been able to survive the ambush in the back of the barbershop in Culver Flats. He only hoped that whoever the judge sent would have the good sense to identify himself before trying to brace him. Reaves could ill afford to give a stranger too much time these days.

In Selma he had found another thread that he hoped would lead to Jim Webb. So far the threads he'd followed had led nowhere—but he was determined to continue his search, a search for which there could be only one end.

Death—Jim Webb's or his own.

TWENTY-TWO

Clint knocked on Maxim's door early the next morning, about an hour before dawn. When Maxim opened it he stared groggily out into the hall.

"What the—"

"Early start, remember?"

"Early, yeah, but—"

"Come on, get dressed and meet me downstairs in ten minutes."

"No breakfast?"

"We'll get breakfast in the next town."

"But—"

"You can have some jerky on the trail," Clint said. "I made arrangements with the liveryman to have our horses ready, with some supplies."

"What's the big rush?"

"I want to get out of here before those three from last night even wake up."

Rubbing his eyes, Maxim asked, "Why are you worried about them? We can handle them."

"I don't want to have to handle anybody, Al," Clint said. "Let's go, I want to beat first light."

"All right, all right, I'm comin'," Maxim moaned,

"but I'm warning you, I can't ride in a straight line when I'm asleep."

"Don't worry," Clint said. "The horses will be awake."

Maxim closed the door and Clint went down to the lobby to wait. He walked to the front door and looked outside. Good, there was nobody in sight. Next he went over to the desk clerk and said, "Is my bill ready?"

Clint had the bill paid by the time Maxim came down the stairs carrying his rifle and saddlebags.

Half an hour before first light Fletcher woke up. He didn't have to dress because he'd fallen asleep that way. He strapped on his gun, grabbed his hat and his gear, and left his room. He went down the hall and banged on the door of Sherman and Masters's room.

"Come on," he shouted, "I want to get to the livery before they do."

The plan he had in mind was easy. Be waiting for them at the livery and knock the deputy unconscious before anybody knew what was going on. After that the three of them could handle Adams.

By first light, Dirk Fletcher would be the man who had killed the Gunsmith—and maybe he'd go ahead and notch the deputy, for good measure.

"Jesus," Maxim said, as he and Clint rode out of town, "it ain't even light."

"That's the point."

"I don't understand why you're avoidin' those three," Maxim said. "How'd you get your reputation doin' that?"

"First of all," Clint said, "if I'd started doing this earlier maybe I wouldn't have this reputation."

"You don't *want* your—"

"And second of all," he went on, cutting Maxim off,

"you're wearing a badge and you've got to live up to it."

"If you knew how many men Judge Parker's deputies bring back slung over their saddles—"

"I do know how many, Al," Clint said. "Why do you think I never accepted the judge's offer of a badge?"

"Well, I figure you didn't *need* his badge, not with your rep—and what did you mean, maybe you wouldn't have this rep? You sound like you're *sorry* you're the Gunsmith."

"A reputation," Clint said, "is not all it's cracked up to be, Al."

Maxim shook his head, still unable to understand, and Clint wasn't in the mood to try to explain it. He wanted to put good distance between them and Culver Flats before first light, so he kicked Duke lightly in the ribs to get him going, and Maxim had to hustle his horse along to keep up.

When Fletcher, Masters, and Sherman reached the livery, Fletcher got a bad feeling.

"What is it?" Sherman asked. He may not have been smart, but he'd ridden with Fletcher long enough to be able to sense his moods.

"Somethin's wrong," Fletcher said.

"Wha—" Masters started, but Fletcher was already running into the livery.

"They're gone!" he shouted.

Masters and Sherman were about to run into the livery, but Fletcher came running out again.

"Goddamn it, they're gone."

"Are you sure?" Sherman asked.

"Their horses are gone!"

"They must have left earlier than they said," Masters remarked.

"You're brilliant!" Fletcher said with disdain.

"Well," Sherman said, "I guess we chalk that one up to a missed opportunity."

"The hell we will," Fletcher said. "Saddle up, boys. We're goin' after them! I'm not lettin' this chance get away from me that easy!"

Fletcher started into the livery, but Masters and Sherman didn't follow.

"What's wrong with you?" he demanded.

"Why go after them?" Sherman asked.

"Why look for trouble, Fletch?" Masters asked.

"Yeah," Sherman said. "They're gone. Forget 'em."

"Do you realize who that was?" Fletcher demanded.

"Yeah," Masters said, "we do."

"The Gunsmith," Sherman said. "Face facts, Fletch. He could probably kill all three of us by himself—and he ain't by himself."

"Why go looking for trouble?" Masters said again.

Fletcher bit his lip. What they said made sense. Much as he'd like to think he could take the Gunsmith, it was a long shot at best.

But he didn't want them to know that.

"Aw, what's the use?" he said. "I ain't gonna go after them alone. If you two had any nerve . . ."

"Come on, Fletch," Sherman said. "We got nerve enough to buy you breakfast."

TWENTY-THREE

As Jim Webb rode into Colton, in Indian Territory, he had an advantage over Bass Reaves—Webb knew there was someone on his trail, and he knew who it was. He'd heard of Deputy Marshal Bass Reaves and knew the black man's reputation. It impressed him, but he felt no fear of the man. He was leading Reaves a merry chase simply because it suited him to do so. It amused him. Eventually, however, he knew that Reaves would catch up to him, and then he'd learn firsthand if the man's reputation was earned or overblown.

Of late, though, he'd decided that it would be better to face Reaves in a place of his choosing, and not someplace at random. Riding into Colton, where he had friends, he thought that perhaps this should be the place.

He rode to the livery and left his horse there, and then instead of going straight to the hotel with his gear he went to the Colton House Saloon, which was owned by his friend and former partner Anson Blake. Blake had made enough money several years ago from a score they'd made together to retire from the outlaw business and open up this saloon and gambling house. He also had rooms upstairs which he rented out to his best customers—or to ex-partners, of which he had one.

Webb entered the saloon, which at this early hour of the afternoon was not doing a brisk business. In fact, in the whole place there were only two men, the bartender, and one man sitting at a table nursing a beer. Webb walked to the bar and dropped his saddlebags on it.

"Beer," he said to the bartender, who, although Webb had been to the Colton House before, he did not know.

"Comin' up."

The bartender brought him the beer and set it down next to the saddlebags.

"Blake around?"

"Who wants to know?"

The bartender was a dark-haired man, swarthy and overweight, but with the huge arms of an ex-fighter or wrestler.

"Jim Webb."

Webb saw the recognition in the man's eyes.

"I'll tell him."

"Thanks."

Webb watched as the barkeep came around the bar and walked to a door in the back of the room. He knocked and went in, and when he came out moments later he was trailed by Anson Blake.

Blake was Webb's age, thirty-five. He'd always been a tall, well-built, handsome man, but Webb saw that the easy life had caused him to gain some weight around the middle. He was still handsome, though, and he had impeccable taste in women. Webb knew he'd have some beautiful ones working for him, and he intended to pick one out for his own use.

He smiled as he approached Webb and stuck out his hand.

"Hello, Jim."

"Anse."

The two men shook hands as the bartender reclaimed his place behind the bar.

"Just get in?"

"Just now," Webb said, slapping his saddlebags. "Haven't even had a chance to look for a room."

This was a charade they went through whenever Webb came to town. Usually Blake's reply was, "You don't have to find a room. You're staying here." Today, however, he was oddly silent.

"I thought you might have a room available," Webb said, prompting his friend.

"Ordinarily, I would have, Jim."

"Ordinarily?"

Blake leaned on the bar. Webb studied the cut of the man's clothes, his expensive trousers and jacket, the boiled white shirt, and he didn't see the outline of a gun anywhere. It either wasn't there, or the tailoring of the jacket was perfect.

"I understand you've got some trouble."

"No more than usual, Anse," Webb replied. "The kind you and I used to handle all the time."

"That's just it, Jim," Blake said. "I don't handle trouble well anymore."

"What are we talkin' about here, Anse?"

"Bass Reaves."

"What about him?"

"I hear he's on your trail."

"So he is."

"You figure to wait for him and face him here?" Blake asked.

"I haven't decided," Webb said. "Why?"

"You wouldn't expect me to be backin' your play, would you?"

Webb thought the question over.

"Are you past it, Anse?"

Blake touched his newly formed girth and said, "Way past handlin' the kind of trouble Bass Reaves would be bringin' with him."

"Are you sayin' I can't stay here?"

"I was just askin' if you expected me to back your play, Jim."

"I never expect anyone to handle my trouble, Anse," Webb said. "I always figure on handling it myself."

Blake grinned in relief at that and asked, "Your regular room okay?"

TWENTY-FOUR

When Bass Reaves received word that Jim Webb might be in the town of Colton, he had no idea that the word had actually been passed by Webb himself. After a week in town Webb had decided that this was where he'd stand against Reaves. Even though his old partner wouldn't back him, he had found a couple of men who would. All that remained now was to sit and wait for Reaves to arrive.

When Reaves got the word about Colton he headed there immediately. At his best speed, though, it would still take him the better part of three days to get there.

Clint waited outside the telegraph office in Selma. Maxim was inside, sending a message to Fort Smith and Judge Parker. A progress report, he called it. Clint called it a "no progress" report.

They had finally picked up Bass Reaves's trail again and it had led them here to Selma. Unfortunately, they were still two, maybe three days behind him. Reaves, being a big black man with a badge, was not hard to notice, so they knew he had been in Selma. A conversation with the local law revealed that the black deputy had caused no trouble. He had eaten, slept, and left the next morning.

When Maxim came out of the telegraph office he was frowning.

"Did he reply right away?"

"Yeah, he did."

"What did he say? Does he want you to go back to Fort Smith?"

"No," Maxim said, handing Clint the telegram. "He wants us to go to Colton."

"Where's that?" Clint scanned the telegram, and it did, indeed, instruct them to go to a town called Colton.

"North," Maxim said, "about three days from here, maybe less."

"Why Colton?"

"That's just it," Maxim said. "You've got it in your hands. That's all it says. Just to go there, no why about it."

"He must have some information," Clint said. "Maybe Reaves is there."

"Or maybe Webb is there."

"That could be, too."

Now it was Clint's turn to frown.

"What's wrong?"

"I'm just wondering. If Webb is in Colton, who sent out the word?"

"Somebody who doesn't like him."

"Or maybe he did it himself."

"Why would he?"

"Maybe he's tired of having Reaves dogging his trail."

"I get it," Maxim said. "You think he's setting a trap for Bass."

"I think it's a possibility," Clint said.

"If that's the case, maybe we better get a move on," Maxim said. "We're gonna want to be there to help him, ain't we?"

"We sure are."

• • •

Anson Blake sat in his office behind his desk, staring unhappily at the wall. Colton had long been his hide-away, the place he had found where he could get away from his past. Now Jim Webb was in town and had not only brought the memories with him, but had actually brought the past with him. The only relationship Blake had had with a lawman for years was with whoever was sheriff of Colton at the time. These days it was a man named Mark Slaten, a decent man who made a good small-town sheriff. He was not, however, equipped to handle Jim Webb and the trouble Webb was bringing to Colton.

Blake knew the reputation of Bass Reaves, and knew that if the black marshal was coming to Colton then only one of them—Reaves or Webb—was going to leave town alive.

There was a knock on the door at that point and Blake said, "Come in."

The door opened and Mark Slaten entered. The sheriff was in his thirties, not inexperienced with life, but certainly inexperienced at dealing with the likes of a Jim Webb, or a Bass Reaves, or even with the kind of man Anson Blake used to be.

"I got word you wanted to talk to me," Slaten said.

"I do," Blake said, "but I would have come to your office."

Slaten waved a hand and said, "I was making rounds, anyway."

"Drink?"

"No, thanks. What can I do for you?"

Slaten was a tall, broad-shouldered man who was very good at handling drunks and disorderly people. He rarely, if ever, had to draw his gun to handle those prob-lems. Blake had no idea how good, or bad, Mark Slaten was with a handgun.

"I wanted to talk to you about Jim Webb."

"Your friend."

Blake hedged.

"We were friends . . . once."

"Not anymore?"

"Do you know what Webb is?"

"Sure," Slaten said, "I wouldn't be any good at my job if I didn't know who and what the Jim Webbs of the world are."

"I used to be like him."

"I know that, too, Anson, but you're not anymore."

"No, I'm not," Blake said, "but I want to warn you about him."

"I don't think I need to be warned—"

"I think you do," Blake insisted. "Bass Reaves is after him."

"I've heard that, too."

"And you intend to let Webb stay here?"

Slaten spread his hands in a helpless gesture.

"He hasn't done anything I can use to make him leave . . . yet."

"So you're watching him?"

"I'm keeping an eye on him, yes."

"Well, that's good."

"I appreciate your concern, Anson," Slaten said, "but I do know how to do my job."

"I wasn't implying that you didn't," Blake said, even though they both knew he was . . . when it came to a Jim Webb.

"If that's all," Slaten said, "I'll continue my rounds."

"That's all I had to say, Mark," Blake said. "Thanks for stopping by."

Slaten left and Blake stared at the door which had closed behind him. The sheriff was a good, decent man.

He had no chance in hell of dealing effectively with Jim Webb.

TWENTY-FIVE

Jim Webb watched from the window as Sheriff Slaten left the saloon and crossed the street. It was barely afternoon; what would the sheriff be doing in the saloon?

"Honey," the girl in his bed called out, "come back to bed. I'm cold."

He turned and looked at the woman. She wasn't a whore—or so she claimed—but by the end of his first day in town she was in his bed. Of the three women Anse Blake had working for him, Marie Ridgeway was the one who had appealed to him the most. She was a big brunette, big in ways that were useful in bed. She had large, round breasts that were not as firm as they once were, and a big butt that was always warm. In fact she was a big, warm, comfortable woman who had an appetite that went with the rest of her—big. She was not fat at all, but compared to the other two girls who worked for Blake, who were both thin—though one of them, Tina, had breasts like ripe peaches—Marie was the one he had imagined in bed, and it was because he knew she'd be warm and cushiony.

He turned and walked back to the bed. He was naked, so she reached out and stroked his penis, which twitched beneath her touch.

''You're such a pretty man,'' she cooed.

''Tell me about the sheriff.''

''What?'' She wasn't sure she had heard right.

''Tell me about the sheriff,'' he said again, ''but don't stop doing what you're doin'.''

She stared at him for a moment with a puzzled look, then shrugged and continued to stroke and fondle him as she spoke.

''What do you want to know about Sheriff Slaten?''

''What kind of man is he?''

''He's a nice man.''

''Nice?'' he asked. ''What about the kind of lawman he is?''

''He's . . . okay.''

''Is he strong?''

''He looks strong.''

''I mean,'' Webb said, ''is he a hard man, does he enforce the law?''

''He enforces the law, but I wouldn't say he was a hard man.''

''A tough man?''

''No.''

''Easy to get along with?''

''If you want to know about Mark Slaten,'' she said, ''you should ask Tina.''

''Is she sleepin' with him?''

''Yep.''

''Okay, then,'' he said, reaching down to touch her head, ''I will talk to Tina . . . but later.''

''And are we through talkin'?'' she asked.

He moved his hand to the back of her head and pushed her toward him.

''Yeah,'' he said, ''we're through.''

''Good.''

There was something else Webb had liked about Marie right away. Her mouth. She had full, soft-looking lips, and he had immediately imagined them moving over his body.

She took his penis in her hand, hard now, guided it to her mouth and slid her lips over him. He moaned as he glided into her hot mouth and she began to suck on him, moaning, fondling his balls at the same time. They'd had sex just half an hour ago, when they had awakened together, but he was ready again, and Marie Ridgeway was *always* ready.

That was something else he liked about her.

When Mark Slaten got to the other side of the street he turned and looked at the second floor of Blake's saloon just in time to see a man move away from the window. He had, indeed, been watching Jim Webb since the man arrived in town, and he knew which room he was in.

Maybe now Jim Webb was watching him, too.

TWENTY-SIX

When Clint and Maxim came within sight of Colton they reined in their horses.

"Not very big," Maxim said.

"Doesn't have to be, I guess," Clint said. "In fact, that might be why Webb picked it."

Clint had managed to convince himself that Jim Webb was laying a trap for Bass Reaves. Why else would the man have been able to elude the black lawman for so long, only to have word get to Judge Parker that he was in Colton?

"I wonder if Webb would face Bass alone," Maxim said.

"I don't think so."

"Why not?"

"His kind never do," Clint said. "They may travel alone from time to time, but they do their robbing and killing and fighting in packs."

"So he's probably got himself some friends in town."

"I'd say that's for sure."

"Well, we might as well ride in and see what we can see," Maxim suggested.

He started his horse forward, but Clint reached out and grabbed the animal's head.

"What's the matter?" Maxim asked.

"We forgot something."

"What?"

"Your badge."

"What about it?"

"You'd better take it off," Clint said, "or you'll be a moving target once we ride into town."

"Judge Parker says we ain't never supposed to take it off," Maxim said.

"Judge Parker's not here, Al," Clint said. "You are, and I am, and Jim Webb may be, and I don't intend to get killed because I'm riding next to a deputy marshal from Judge Parker's court. Take it off, or turn around and go back to Fort Smith."

"Well," Maxim said, "when you put it that way."

He unpinned the badge from his chest and started to put it in his shirt pocket.

"Your saddlebag would be a better place."

Maxim shrugged and transferred the badge to his saddlebag.

"Happy?"

Clint released his horse's head and said, "Very. Let's go."

Even though Clint had made Maxim remove his badge he still intended to visit the local law and have a talk with him. He'd be the only one in town who would know that Maxim was a deputy marshal.

However, they did not ride up to the sheriff's office when they saw it. They continued past until they found the livery. Once the horses were taken care of, they went looking for a hotel. Once their gear was stored in their rooms, they left the hotel and walked to the sheriff's office. Clint had made Maxim take the badge out again and put it in his pocket this time, so they'd have it to show the local sheriff. He ignored the man's remark about "making up your mind."

When they entered the sheriff's office Clint made the initial introductions.

"I've heard of you, Adams," Mark Slaten said, shaking hands with Clint, then looking at Maxim. "But do you have a badge to go with your name?"

Maxim produced the badge from his pocket, then returned it.

"You can send a wire to Fort Smith if you want to check on him," Clint said.

"Why aren't you wearing your badge, Deputy?"

Clint hoped Maxim wouldn't say it was because he had told him not to.

"Didn't want to be a moving target."

"For who?"

"Jim Webb."

They could see from the sheriff's face that he knew the name.

"Is he here, in town?" Clint asked.

"He is."

"And you haven't arrested him?" Maxim asked.

"I don't have anything to arrest him for, Deputy."

"How about murder?"

"He hasn't killed anyone in Colton, and that's all I'm concerned with. If you want to arrest him, then you do it—or are you waiting for Bass Reaves to show up?"

"How do you know about Reaves?" Clint asked.

Slaten laughed shortly.

"Everybody in town knows that Webb is waiting for Reaves."

"And what were you gonna do when Bass got to town?" Maxim asked. "Watch?"

Slaten fixed Maxim with a hard stare and said, "I was going to do my job—and I still intend to. Unless, like I said, you want to arrest him. I'm sure between the two of you, you can handle him."

"Do you know if Webb has picked up any friends in town?" Clint asked.

"He already had one in place when he got here," Slaten said. "His name's Anson Blake, and he owns a saloon."

"Were they partners?" Clint asked.

"How'd you know that? Recognize the name?"

"No," Clint said, "but I think the only way a man like Jim Webb can meet friends is if he worked with them, once."

"Well, yeah, they did once, but Blake's put all that behind him."

"Then why's he helping Webb now?" Maxim asked.

"He's not," Slaten insisted. "He's only givin' him a place to stay."

"Well," Maxim said, "in my book, that's helpin' him."

"Well, Deputy," Sheriff Slaten said, "I guess you and me just operate from a different book, don't we?"

TWENTY-SEVEN

Outside the sheriff's office, Clint said, "Well, that didn't accomplish much."

"What did you think it would accomplish?"

"Well, I thought maybe we'd get the sheriff on our side."

"You sayin' it's my fault we didn't?"

Clint nodded.

"That's what I'm saying."

"Well . . . maybe you're right. What do you want to do now?"

"I don't know."

"Should I arrest Webb?"

"You want to try that?"

"With you to back me, sure."

"Before we try that we'll have to find out who he's got backing his play," Clint said. "We can't walk into a crowded saloon without knowing who to look at."

"So how do we do that?"

"One of two ways," Clint said. "We can watch him and see who his friends are."

"Or?"

"Or we can ask him."

"What about a third way?"

"And what would that be?"

"Asking this fella Blake, who used to be his partner," Maxim said.

Clint gave Maxim the kind of look a proud father would give a son.

"You know," he said, "that's a sound idea."

Maxim almost pouted and said, "You don't have to sound so surprised."

"Let's find this fella Blake."

"Which saloon does he own?"

"I don't know the name of it," Clint said, "but maybe there's only one in town. There's only *one* way we're going to find that out."

They walked around town and found out that there were two saloons in town. They went inside the first one they found and asked if it was owned by Anson Blake. When they were told it wasn't they continued on and found the second one.

"Yeah," the bartender said, "it is." The man had the look of an ex-fighter. "Who wants to know?"

"Tell him Clint Adams."

If the man recognized the name he didn't show it.

"Wait here."

They waited while the man announced Clint, and then Anson Blake put in his appearance. He looked like a once handsome young man who had gone to seed. He was well dressed, though.

"Clint Adams?" he said, approaching the bar. The saloon wasn't busy, and he must have known the other men who were standing at the bar already.

"That's right."

"The Gunsmith?"

Clint nodded.

"Well, this is a real pleasure."

Blake put out this hand and Clint shook it.

"This is my friend, Al Maxim."

"Mr. Maxim," Blake said, but didn't offer to shake hands. "What brings you to my place?"

"We just rode into town and we wanted to ask you a few questions."

"Me? Questions?" Blake asked. "About what?"

"Not what," Clint said, "who. We want to talk to you about Jim Webb."

Blake froze for a moment, then asked carefully, "What about him?"

"Is there someplace we can talk," Clint asked, "privately?"

Blake hesitated, then said, "Sure, my office. Just come this way."

They followed Blake to his office, where he sat behind his desk without offering them a drink or asking them to sit down. He seemed more secure there, with the desk between them.

"Which one of you is the law?" he asked.

Maxim took out his badge and showed it to him.

"I thought Bass Reaves was the deputy who was after Webb."

"He is," Maxim said.

"Then why are you both here?"

"To keep Webb from closing a trap on Reaves."

"Trap?" Blake asked. "What trap?"

"You don't know?"

"I don't know anything about a trap."

"But you know Webb."

"Sure, I do."

"In fact, you once rode with him."

"So?"

"He's staying here, isn't he?"

"You must know all of this already," Webb said. "Why don't you ask me something you don't know?"

"And if we do, will we get a straight answer?" Clint asked.

"Only one way to find out," Blake said.

It seemed to Maxim that he was hearing that a lot lately.

TWENTY-EIGHT

"Webb is waiting here for Reaves, isn't he?" Clint
asked.

"Yes."

"Are you set to back his play?"

"No."

"Why not? You're friends, aren't you?"

"That's not such an easy question to answer yes or
no," Blake said.

"Why not? You either are friends, or you aren't,"
Clint said. "What's so hard about that?"

"We were friends when we were ... working together ... at least, I think we were."

"And now?"

"And now I know we're not."

"But you're letting him stay here."

"We *used* to be friends," Blake said, as if he was
suddenly certain of that now. "That's got to count for
something."

"Let me ask you something."

"What?"

"Did you ever trust Webb?"

"How do you mean? With my life?"

111

"No," Clint said, "with money. Did you ever trust that after a job he wouldn't cheat you?"

Blake thought a moment, then said, "No."

"Then how can you say you were friends?" Maxim asked.

"Webb would cheat his friends," Blake said. "He'd have no problem with that. Besides, I said we were friends . . . kind of."

"Blake," Clint said, "has Webb found anyone to back his play?"

"Yes."

"Who?"

"A few men."

"What are their names?"

Blake didn't speak.

"Are *they* your friends?" Clint asked.

"No."

"Then why not tell us?"

"I've told you too much already."

"Are you afraid of Webb?" Clint asked.

"You're damned right I am. I was afraid of him when we rode together, when I was *like* him. Now I'm a different man, and I'm even more afraid of him."

Clint and Maxim exchanged a look, and then Clint said, "Well, I guess you've told us enough. If we watch Webb long enough he'll lead us to his new friends."

Blake didn't comment on that. He sat with his mouth in a tight, thin line, as if he was holding back any further words.

"We'll leave now, Blake," Clint said.

"Yeah," Maxim said sarcastically, "thanks for talking to us."

They walked to the door of the office, where Clint stopped and turned back.

"Well," he said, "if it's any consolation, I think you've already told us enough to get you killed."

He and Maxim left. When they did Anson Blake sat with his head in his hands for a very long time.

"Did you believe him?" Maxim asked.

"Every word he said."

"Why?"

"Because he was too scared to lie," Clint said. "Unfortunately, he wasn't too scared to shut up on us at the end. I'd be more interested in what he didn't say."

"Think he'll tell Webb we're here?"

Clint rubbed his nose as he thought that one over.

"That's a hard one to answer. He might be too scared not to tell him."

"Can we get a beer before we leave here?" Maxim asked. "Talking to people is thirsty work."

"Sure," Clint said, "maybe Webb will even come down from his room and we'll catch him alone."

Maxim looked around the room. There were enough men there that one or two of them could have been there to watch Webb's back.

"Like you said," he commented as they walked to the bar, "we got to find out who his backup is first."

They walked to the bar and ordered two beers from the brawny bartender.

"You gents law?" he asked as he set the beers down. His mouth barely moved.

"That's right," Maxim said, before Clint could stop him. Once a bartender knew something the whole town usually heard about it.

"Lookin' for Jim Webb?"

"Yes," Clint said.

"He's upstairs."

"Right now?" Maxim asked.

The man nodded.

"What room?" Clint asked.

"Four," the man said, "overlooking the street."

"Thanks," Clint said. The bartender nodded and moved away.

"Why's he so helpful?" Maxim asked.

"Maybe he wants to help his boss."

"And maybe he wants us to walk into a trap."

"Maybe we should just drink our beers and get out of here for a while."

"That I agree with," Maxim said.

TWENTY-NINE

Bass Reaves could not believe his bad luck. His horse had stepped in a chuckhole and snapped his right foreleg. He'd had to put it out of its misery, and then carry his saddle and belongings ten miles to the nearest town. Once there nobody would sell him a horse. Finally, someone had told him that there was a rancher outside of town who didn't care whom he sold horses to. "Even niggers." Reaves had to walk two more miles to reach the ranch.

As he approached the ranch he realized it was a small spread. The house had obviously been built by someone who knew what he was doing but didn't have much money. Similarly, the nearby corral was sturdy and more than able to contain the half a dozen or so horses that were inside at the time.

He was several yards from the house when the door opened and a woman stepped out. She was holding a rifle and pointed it at him.

"What do you want?"

Reaves was kind of breathless from all the walking he had done that day. He stopped and took a moment to try to catch his breath.

"Well?"

He stared at the woman. She was in her early thirties, tall and well built, with dark hair pinned up on her head. He thought if she had her face painted up like the women in saloons and whorehouses did she'd be real pretty. She held the rifle as if she knew how to use it.

"Ma'am," he said, "I jest walked ten miles to town, and then from town to here, all the while carrying this here saddle and rifle and saddlebags."

"What happened to your horse?"

"It stepped in a chuckhole and I had to put it out of its misery. You min' if I put this stuff down?"

She thought a moment, then said, "No, go ahead."

He saw a water pump to his right.

"And would you min' if I got some water from that pump, there?"

"Go ahead."

He walked to the pump and ignored the tin cup sitting on it. He didn't know how the woman would react to a black man using her cup. He'd just stick his head under the mouth of the pump and drink.

"Why don't you use the cup?" she asked.

"It's all right, ma'am," he said, "I don't have to use—"

"You go ahead and use the cup," she said. "I ain't holdin' this gun on ya because you're black; it's because you're a stranger."

"Yes, ma'am," he said, "and I can't say as I blame you. Thank you, ma'am, I'll use the cup."

"Stop callin' me ma'am," she said as he filled the cup and drank deeply. As he tipped it back to drain it she saw the badge.

"You a lawman?"

"Yes, ma—yes, I am. A deputy marshal from Judge Parker's court in Fort Smith."

She lowered the rifle.

"Well, why didn't you say so? You must be hungry

after all that walkin'. Come inside and I'll fix you something to eat.''

"Ma'am, is your husband home?''

"No, he ain't,'' she said, ''and I don't know when he will be. He's on a trail drive and he's been gone for a month, likely be gone another month. That don't mean you can't come in, though. You can leave that saddle out on the porch.''

"Yes, ma—''

"My name's Brenda,'' she said. ''You can call me that, okay?''

"Yes . . . Brenda.''

"And your name?''

"Reaves,'' he said, ''Bass Reaves.''

"Well, Marshal Reaves,'' she said, ''you come on inside and I'll fix you somethin' hot.''

"I'm much obliged, Brenda,'' he said. ''I truly am.''

THIRTY

She fixed him a wonderful home-cooked meal, the likes of which he hadn't seen in years. Chicken, dumplings, corn bread, the best coffee he'd ever had, and then after dinner—which she shared with him—she brought out a bottle of whiskey.

"You are one mighty fine cook, Brenda," he told her, sitting back in his chair feeling as if he was going to burst. "Your husband is a fool to stay away for so long."

"He is for more reasons than you know, Bass," she said, regarding him from across the table with an odd look on her face.

"How do you mean?"

"I mean cookin' ain't all I'm good at, if you catch my drift."

Reaves shook his head. She couldn't mean what he thought she meant, could she?

"Maybe I'm jest bein' dense—"

"No, you're not," she said. "You know what I mean. I have appetites, Bass, appetites that go unsatisfied while my husband is away."

"Brenda, I don't think we should be talkin'—"

"About sex?" she asked. "Why not?"

"Well, you're married—"

"And you're black and I'm white?"

"Well, there's that—"

"Have you ever been with a white woman, Bass?"

"No, I haven't—"

"Ever wonder about us?"

"Brenda—"

"Come on, you can say yes without me thinkin' you're wicked, or a rapist, or somethin'."

"Brenda—"

" 'Cause I'm sure wonderin' about you, Bass."

He didn't know what to say.

"Mind you, I'm not sayin' I've always wondered about black men, but I'm wonderin' about you. Have been since you first walked up to the house."

"Brenda—"

"Have you ever seen a naked white woman?"

"No—"

"No? You haven't been to whorehouses?"

"Well, yes, but—"

"Here," she said, and suddenly she unbuttoned the top of her gingham dress and pulled it down from her shoulders. Her breasts seemed to burst free and she took them in her hands and held them up to him, as if they were two overripe fruits—which is what they looked like. They were pale, with dark brown nipples, and as she squeezed them they swelled in her hands. Sitting there looking at her holding her breasts in her hands was possibly the most erotic thing he'd ever seen in his life.

"How do you like them?"

He swallowed and said, "They're right pretty."

"Yes, they are," she said. "Even I think so. So you see, these are two more reasons my husband shouldn't be leavin' me alone."

"Oh, I agree."

"Take a closer look," she said. She got up and came around to his side of the table. "Scoot your chair back."

He did as he was told, and she plopped down in his lap. She held her warm breasts to his face and he closed his eyes and felt the smooth skin with his lips.

"Bite me, Bass," she said huskily, "come on, bite my nipples."

"Yes, ma'am," he said, and she didn't even scold him for calling her ma'am again. He bit her nipples, first one and then the other, and then he sucked them and licked them while she moaned and opened her dress the rest of the way. She squirmed in his lap, feeling his erection beneath her fanny.

"Oh, my," she said, wiggling her butt, "we've got to get that out of there, don't we?"

She slid from his lap, got to her knees, and undid his pants. He lifted his hips so she could pull them down and his erection jumped out at her, hard and pulsing.

"Oh, my, yes," she said, and took it in both her hands. She rubbed her fingertips over the smooth-as-glass skin, then leaned forward and ran her tongue over him. "Mmmm, you taste just fine, don't you?"

"I don't—" About then he stopped and caught his breath as her mouth swooped down and took him inside. She held him firmly in both hands and bobbed her head up and down, sucking him wetly, moaning the whole time. Then, abruptly, she released him, stood up, and held on to him with one hand. He had no choice but to stand up.

"Come on," she said, "the bed's in here."

"Brenda—"

"Hush up, Bass Reaves," she said. "You owe me for the meal I just gave you."

Her dress had fallen down to her waist and he could see that she was pale and smooth all over. She tugged him along, leading him to the bedroom.

"I jest . . . jest came by to buy a horse," he said as she led him to the bed.

"Sit down," she said, pushing him down. She pulled

his boots off, and then his pants. "We can talk about a horse tomorrow."

"Tomorrow?"

"That's right."

She took off his shirt and ran her hands over his chest.

"My God, you're the hardest man I've ever seen," she said. "I'll bet you're a tough man, too, aren't you?"

"Yes, ma—"

"But not so tough with me, are you?"

She took his penis in her hands and again pumped it. He lifted his hips and groaned as she slid one hand down his shaft so she could cup his heavy balls, and then leaned over and began to suck him again. He reached for her head and held it. It had been a long time since he'd been with a woman and he was afraid she was going to finish him too quickly, but she released him and said, "Oh, no, not yet. You have to last awhile longer."

She pushed him so that he was lying on the bed, and he watched as she peeled her dress off the rest of the way. His eyes went to the black tangle of hair between her legs, and he could smell how wet and ready she was.

She got on the bed with him, straddled him, raised herself up and then lowered herself down on him, taking him inside slowly, inch by agonizing inch, both of them moaning and groaning with each inch until she was sitting down on him and he was nestled up into her nice and deep and tight.

"Ummm," she said, "now . . ." and she began riding him up and down, slowly at first, and then more quickly as he watched her lush breasts bobbing about with every move.

"You came looking for a horse," she said, laughing, "but I'm the one gettin' the ride!"

THIRTY-ONE

The hotel Clint and Maxim were staying in had a small dining room and they decided to have breakfast there the next morning.

"Webb might know about us by now," Maxim said, "if Blake told him."

"I thought about that last night," Clint said. "I don't think Blake will tell him."

"Why not?"

"Because he probably figures we'll take care of Webb for him."

"Kill him?"

"Get him out of town, at least," Clint said. "If Blake has really put that life behind him—and I believe that he has—then he's probably not going to do anything beyond giving Webb a room."

"He wouldn't tell us who Webb got to back his play against Bass."

"I think he'd tell us today, if we asked him again," Clint said. "I think he spent the night thinking about it, like we did—"

"I went to the local whorehouse," Maxim said with a grin. "You stayed in your room and thought about this."

123

"Didn't run into Webb there, did you?"

"Not that I know of," Maxim said. "Fact is, I don't know what Webb looks like."

"Neither do I," Clint said. "That's going to have to be the first thing we correct today."

"After breakfast," Maxim said as the waiter came to the table with their steak and eggs.

"Right," Clint said, "after breakfast."

Jim Webb looked down at Tina, who was in his bed this morning instead of Marie. He'd told Marie that he was tired and was going to go sleep. She pouted, but when he pointed out that she was a lot of woman, and he needed some rest if he was going to keep up with her, she smiled and told him to sleep well. Then he'd gone upstairs, where Tina was waiting for him.

Although Tina was sleeping with the sheriff on her own time, she was still for rent, and Webb had rented her for the night. She wasn't as meaty as Marie was, the way he usually liked his women, but she had something Marie didn't have and that was the firmest breasts he'd ever come across. They were, indeed, like two peaches that hadn't quite ripened yet. Webb had spent a lot of time on them during the night, licking them, sucking the nipples, because he had never before run across a woman so firm. He knew, though, that this night with Tina would just make Marie's breasts seem that much softer and more comfortable.

But a man does need some variety.

He woke Tina by sliding his hand down between her legs and rubbing her until she was awake and wet. Then he straddled her and fucked her hard until he exploded, not at all worried about whether she was satisfied or not.

"You're a lot of man, Webb," she said later.

"Save the phony talk for the customers that need it, Tina," he said, slipping on his pants. "Come on, I want

some breakfast and I ain't leavin' you in my room while
I get it.''

"Are you afraid I'll steal something?''

She looked up at him from the bed, her pretty little
face and eyes staring up at him from beneath an absolute
waterfall of honey-blond hair.

"Won't you?''

"My boyfriend is the sheriff, you know. I wouldn't
steal anything.''

He'd been waiting all night for her to say something
like that.

"The sheriff?''

"That's right.''

"Hey,'' Webb said, "he's not gonna come after me,
is he?''

"For what?''

"For bein' with you.''

She waved a hand and said, "He knows what I do to
make money.''

"Oh, he's understanding, huh?''

"Sure is.''

"Not jealous?''

"Not at all.''

"Is he . . . tough?''

"Oh, no,'' she said, "he's real sweet.''

"Well, to you, maybe,'' Webb said, strapping on his
gun, "but what about when he's workin'? You gotta be
real tough to be a lawman.''

"Not him,'' she said. "In fact, he looks real tough,
but he probably should be a storekeeper instead of a
sheriff.''

"Is that a fact?''

"He knows how to handle drunks and all, but we've
never had a real tough problem here in town.''

"No bank robberies, or anything like that?''

"Who'd want to rob the bank in this town?'' she
asked. "There's nothin' in it.''

"Then I guess he's got no worries," Webb said. "And neither do I. You just take your time lettin' yourself out, Tina."

"Gee, thanks," she said. "I am a little tired. You keep Marie up all night goin' at it like we did?"

"Oh, sure," he said, "but you know what? I don't think you should tell Marie anything about this. Okay?"

"Oh, I get it," Tina said. "She's givin' it to you for free."

"That's right," Webb said, "just like you and your sheriff."

"Well," she said, "with me and him it's probably gonna lead to somethin' more permanent."

"Marriage, huh?"

She nodded.

"As soon as he asks me. Then I can get out of this crummy business—oh, hey, no offense."

"None taken," Webb said. "Do we have a deal? Don't say anythin' to Marie?"

"Sure," Tina said. "We ain't great friends, or nothin', but I ain't lookin' to hurt her feelings none."

"That's good. I appreciate that."

Webb walked to the door. They'd gotten the business part out of the way last night, so he just waved, told her again to take her time, and left.

THIRTY-TWO

Clint and Maxim decided that the bartender at the saloon might not mind pointing Webb out to them, as long as they didn't let on that it was him. The saloon wasn't open yet, though, so they simply took a walk around town. During the walk Maxim told Clint about the girl he'd been with last night.

"She was amazing. Blond, cute as a button, looked about seventeen but I know she was at least twenty or a little more."

"You like them to look young?"

"I like them to be young," Maxim said, "but not that young. After all, I'm not that old, myself."

"I am," Clint said.

"Oh, you're not that old."

"Let's not even talk about it. What was the girl's name?"

"Sheila."

Clint had an idea.

"Who knows almost as much about what goes on in a town as a bartender?" he asked.

"A whore?"

"Right."

"You want me to ask Sheila what she knows?"

"It wouldn't hurt. Maybe she's been with Webb, or maybe with one of the men Webb has recruited. Maybe somebody's been bragging. Men do brag to women, you know. Even to whores."

"They do?" Maxim asked innocently.

"Al," Clint said warningly, "what did you tell her about us?"

"Not much."

"Al . . ."

"I told her I was a deputy," he said. "That impressed her."

"And what about me?"

"What about you?"

Clint put his hand on Maxim's arm to stop him and turned to face him.

"Did you tell her about me?"

"Not really."

"What does 'not really' mean?"

"Well . . . I told her my partner was famous, but I didn't tell her your name."

"My name?"

"That's right."

"Which name?"

"How many names have you got?"

"You know what I mean," Clint said. "Did you say anything about the Gunsmith?"

"No, I didn't . . . I swear! I just told her you were famous, and that I'd come back and tell her more."

"Well," Clint suggested, "why don't you go back and ask her more, instead of telling her more."

"Well," Maxim said as they started walking again, "I'm going to have to tell her something."

"Why?"

"If I don't I'll look like I was just braggin'."

"And?"

"I mean I'll look like a fool."

"A man like you look like a fool to a woman? A whore? Never."

"Clint—"

"We'll think of something for you to tell her," Clint said. "Of course, it may not matter."

"Why not?"

"If Reaves rides in today the whole thing will blow up, anyway. I get the feeling he doesn't plan much, just rushes right in."

"Well," Maxim said, "it helps that he thinks he's bulletproof."

"Nobody's bulletproof."

"He thinks he is."

"Well," Clint said, "let's just hope that we're not around when he finds out he isn't."

THIRTY-THREE

Reaves woke the next morning with Brenda lying on his left arm. He'd spent the entire night with her and didn't know her last name. If her husband walked through the door at that moment, one of them would end up dead—most likely the husband. And if she—a white woman—wanted to start yelling that he—a black man— had raped her, he would be in so much trouble Judge Parker probably wouldn't have been able to get him out of it.

And yet he wasn't sorry he'd done it.

He felt better than he had felt in months, and he knew it was because he had been keeping so much bottled up inside of him. Most of it was anger, a lot of it was frustration. Whatever it was, though, Brenda had helped him work a lot of it off, and for that he was grateful to her.

Webb was still out there, and he was still going to get him, but he thought that now he'd have a better chance of doing it and coming out alive. Now there was less chance of his doing something stupid, because he didn't feel the tension he'd been feeling the past few months. He didn't even feel all the miles he had walked yesterday. He did, however, feel all the miles he and Brenda

131

had put on her bed last night. There was a pleasant fatigue in his groin and in his legs.

Brenda moaned and rolled into him, then opened her eyes and looked up at him.

"I've never had a black man before," she said.

"What did you think?"

She closed her eyes and smiled, ran her hand over his hard chest and stomach and then down between his legs.

"I think it could get to be a habit," she said, stroking him until he was rigid. "Do you have to leave right away?"

"Not right away," he said. "I have time for breakfast."

"Ah," she said, "he wants me to make breakfast."

"And I have to buy a horse."

"Oh, yes," she said, closing her hand around him tightly, "and you can start paying for it right now."

"Again?" he asked.

"Oh, again," she said, using her thumb to rub the spongy head of his penis, "and again, and again . . ."

Suddenly, he thought he knew why her husband stayed away so long. The man couldn't handle her.

But Bass Reaves could.

After breakfast they walked out to the corral together and he picked out a horse.

"Are you sure you won't take any money?" he asked. "It'd be comin' from Judge Parker, not from me."

"No money," she said, "not after yesterday . . . and last night . . . and this morning. You've more than paid for a horse."

"Still—"

"Just keep quiet, Bass Reaves," she said. "Thanks to you I might stay sane until my fool husband comes home again."

He turned and faced her.

"I was thinking the same thing myself, this morning," he said.

"That I was sane?"

"That thanks to you I might stay sane a little longer," he said. "You see, I've been chasing a man for a long time, so long it's turned into an obsession. Now maybe I won't go crazy before I catch him, though."

"And when you do catch him will you kill him?"

"I don't know."

"Or maybe he'll kill you?"

"That's possible, I guess," he said.

"The scars on your body," she said, "I know them well now. Bullets, knives—"

"I've been wounded a few times."

"And whipped."

"That, too."

He looked around.

"Do you have anyone working for you?"

"No."

"No hands?"

"Some temporary ones, but they only come around when Martin—that's my husband—when he's here."

"If you had some men around here—"

"I don't sleep with other men when my husband's away," she said, "not usually."

"I didn't mean—"

"I know, but I want you to know that there wasn't a man before you, and there won't be one after. I want you to believe me."

"I do."

"Why?"

"Because I don't think you'd lie to me."

She looked into the corral.

"Pick one out and take it."

"Brenda," he said, "I have to leave."

"To catch up with your obsession?"

"Yes."

"And after you have?"

"Back to Fort Smith, I guess."

"Maybe you'll pass this way again?"

"Maybe."

"Don't," she said. "It wouldn't be wise, for either of us."

"No," he said, "I guess it wouldn't."

They stood very close for a moment, both touching, and then he said, "Well, I better get that horse."

"Yes," she said, "you better. I'll get you some food to take with you."

He had a horse saddled and had walked it to the house by the time she came out. She handed him a sack with some food in it, and he mounted up, thinking it was still better if they didn't touch again.

"You take care, Bass Reaves."

"I will."

"You better."

"Will you be . . . all right?"

"I'll be fine," she said. "The loving wife waiting for her man to come back."

"Yes."

"Her husband, anyway," she said.

Reaves stared at her a few moments, then turned the horse and rode away. He almost looked back a couple of times, but managed to resist it. When he thought of her he wanted it to be in images from last night—naked, aroused, wild—and not standing there, waving good-bye to him.

THIRTY-FOUR

"That's him."

The bartender's name was Leo. He was pointing out Jim Webb to Clint, who was standing at the bar waiting for Maxim to arrive. Webb was sitting at a table with three other men.

"Who are the other three?" Clint asked. "Locals?"

"One is a local, the other two came into town just before he did."

"Did he know them before, do you think?"

"No," Leo said, "and I only know that because I was here when they met at the bar."

"But they knew who he was."

"Yeah," Leo said, leaning massive forearms on the bar. "They were real impressed when he introduced himself."

"So they were probably only too happy to offer their services to him. What about the local?"

"Fancies hisself a gunman," Leo said. "Worked on one of the ranches near here until Webb recruited him. Name's Bodine. Now, anytime Webb leaves his room he don't go nowhere without them."

"Any others?"

Leo shook his head.

''Far as I know, just those three.''

At that point Maxim came walking in and joined Clint at the bar.

''Beer,'' he said to Leo.

''Comin' up.''

''Webb's in the corner, table with four men. He's the one with his back to the wall.''

Maxim risked a quick look, then turned away.

''What'd you find out from your friend?'' Clint asked.

''She says nobody named Webb has been in there, but a fella named Bodine has.''

''Bodine?''

''Some local who thinks he's a hand with a gun. He's been braggin' that he's workin' with Jim Webb now.''

''Leo just told me about him. Him and the other two sitting with him. Webb doesn't go anywhere without them, except to his room.''

Leo came with Maxim's beer and the lawman accepted it with a nod of thanks.

''So Bass would have been walkin' into four guns,'' he said over the rim of the mug.

''Looks that way.''

''So now what do we do?''

''What we should do is lessen the odds a little.''

''How do we do that?''

''Well, now we know what all of Webb's helpers look like,'' Clint said. ''We'll have to see what they do when he goes to his room.''

''In other words,'' Maxim said, scowling, ''more waiting.''

''Patience is a big part of being a lawman, Al,'' Clint said.

''I'm findin' that out, ain't I?''

''So tell me,'' Clint said, ''what did you have to give your friend Sheila in exchange for the information?''

Maxim smiled at Clint.

''I mean besides that.''

"Oh," Maxim said, "you mean about you."

"Yes," Clint said. "What did you tell her?"

"Well," Maxim said uncomfortably, "I had to tell her something that would impress her."

"Yes."

"And something she'd believe."

"So?"

Maxim hesitated.

"Al, you didn't tell her who I really was, did you?" Clint asked.

"No."

"Then what *did* you tell her?"

Maxim hesitated again, then said without looking at Clint, "I told her you were Wyatt Earp."

"What?"

"I was gonna say Wild Bill Hickok, but I thought she might know he was dead."

"And she believed you?"

"Yep."

"So now everyone in town is going to be looking for Wyatt Earp."

"And not for you."

Now it was Clint's turn to be silent.

"You ain't mad, are you?" Maxim asked.

"No," Clint said, "actually, I kind of like it. People are going to be going nuts trying to get a look at Wyatt Earp, maybe even Webb." Clint smiled. "I like it a lot!"

THIRTY-FIVE

Clint and Maxim never saw Webb without his backup men. In fact, Webb never left the saloon, and the only time he got up from the table he was seated at was to go to his room for the night.

Clint and Maxim remained in the saloon until closing, but Webb's backup men never left their table until closing time. They played a game of poker, just the three of them, and turned away anyone who tried to join.

When the saloon closed Clint thought about following the men to see where they were staying, but the streets were too empty and, although it was dark, there was too much chance they'd be detected.

The only satisfaction they had the whole day was when, during the course of the evening, they heard the Wyatt Earp rumor begin to circulate through the saloon. They even laughed about it on the way back to their hotel.

Outside of their rooms Maxim said, "What do you think the chances are Reaves won't make it here by tomorrow?"

"I thought he'd be here by now," Clint said. "I think it's almost a sure thing—but then I've bet on sure things

before and come up empty. We'll just have to wait and
see.''

They both went into their rooms and went to sleep
for the night.

Jeff Bodine walked to the rooming house with the Ratliff
brothers, listening to them bicker along the way. Sam
and Ben Ratliff were a couple of years apart, ten or
twelve years older than Bodine's twenty-eight, and they
constantly bickered like kids. Bodine, on the other hand,
spoke very infrequently. He preferred to let his gun do
his talking for him.

He tuned out the brothers and wondered when this
black marshal with the big rep was finally going to get
to Colton. Bodine was looking to finally prove what he'd
been telling people in this town for so long, that he was
the fastest gun either side of the Mississippi. Once he
killed that marshal for Jim Webb, he'd have the same
kind of rep Webb had. That was the only reason he put
up with the Ratliff brothers' constant arguing.

"See ya in the mornin', kid," Ben said, as they
reached the boardinghouse and went up the stairs to their
rooms.

"Yeah," Sam said, "in the mornin'."

As Bodine entered his room he heard one of the brothers say to the other one, "Kid gives me the creeps. He
never talks."

Bodine closed his door and smiled. That was the
whole point.

Bass Reaves was making good time with his new horse.
Maybe Brenda's husband didn't know how to treat his
wife, but he apparently knew how to raise horses. The
batch he was selling to the army would probably suit
them just fine, if this one was any indication.

He camped for the night and ate some of the bacon
and beans and biscuits she had packed for him. He

thought about Jim Webb and was glad to see that, although he still wanted to catch the man, he was no longer so . . . intense about it. In fact, even he felt the difference in his face. The mighty scowl he'd been wearing for what seemed like months—and probably was—was gone.

He wondered what Judge Parker's reaction would be when he brought Jim Webb in alive.

Who would have thought that all he needed to do to get rid of his anger was to sleep with a woman? He wondered if any woman would have done as well, or if it had specifically been Brenda, and their situation, that had done the trick for him.

Reaves was not tremendously experienced with women, but Brenda had struck him as an uncommon one. She was obviously married to a fool.

Reaves cleaned his utensils, stowed them in his saddlebags, then rolled himself up in his blanket for the night. With any luck he'd reach the town of Colton by dark the next night—and if he didn't, but was within spitting for distance, he intended to keep riding until he got there.

So, one way or another, he was going to be there tomorrow.

Jim Webb stared out the window at the street and listened to Marie's breathing from the bed behind him. The past hour had confirmed for him that he had made the right decision choosing her over the younger, firmer Tina. Marie was simply more woman, physically and in experience.

Webb thought Reaves would have been in Colton by now, not that he was complaining about having to kill time with Marie. What he didn't like, however, was being stuck in the saloon all day. Tomorrow he just might take a chance on leaving the saloon and taking a turn around town. As long as he had his backup with him, that shouldn't be a problem.

Maybe he'd pay the sheriff a visit. Yeah, Tina's gentle lawman boyfriend. That might even prove to be fun.

THIRTY-SIX

In the morning Clint woke with a bad feeling. He walked to the window and looked outside. There was nothing in sight to support his premonition that it was going to be a bad day, but as he washed and dressed he couldn't shake it.

He stopped at Maxim's room and knocked on the door. The young deputy opened the door, fully dressed.

"You, too?" Maxim asked.

Nothing had impressed Clint about Maxim as much as this question.

"Yeah," he said. "I think we should stay together today."

"I agree."

They went downstairs and had breakfast together.

After breakfast they went out in front of the hotel and spotted three men sitting in front of the saloon.

"That's them," Maxim said. "Bodine and the other two. Waiting to get in, or waiting for Webb to come out."

Clint accepted their presence as part and parcel of the bad day to come.

"What do we do?" Maxim asked.

"Watch them, I guess."

"You guess?"

"We could go after Webb," Clint said, "and go right through them."

"Kill them, you mean?"

"Sure," Clint said. "You take one, I take two, we could probably do it, but why should they die? Because they work for him?"

"No," Maxim said after a moment, "that wouldn't be right."

"No, it wouldn't."

They sat in chairs in front of the hotel, from where they could still see the saloon.

"What if they came after us?" Maxim asked. "What then? Would you kill them?"

"In self-defense, yes, but why would they do that?"

"They'd do it if Webb told them to."

"And why would he do that?"

Maxim took his badge out of his shirt pocket, where he'd been carrying it, and pinned it back on to his shirt. Clint looked at it and said nothing for a moment, then looked down the street at the three men. Leo, the bartender, was opening the front door of the saloon, and the three men went inside.

"Yeah, well," Clint said finally, "that might do it."

They decided to go to the sheriff and tell him that they'd decided to make it known that Maxim was a federal marshal. Before they could leave their chairs, though, Jim Webb suddenly came out of the saloon, with the other three men following.

"Jesus," Maxim said, "he's out."

"What's he doing?" Clint said.

"Who cares," Maxim said. "What matters is that he's out in the open."

"And the other three are still with him."

"We can't take the four of them?"

Clint looked at Maxim.

"Al, the only person I can be sure of is me. I know what I can do. I've never seen Webb, I've never seen the other three, and I don't know what you can do. You tell me. Can we take the four of them?"

Maxim stared at him for a few moments, as if he was going to argue, then looked away.

"I don't know," he said finally. "Webb's supposed to be real good. If it was just the other three I'd say yeah, we can take them. Like you said, I'd take one and you'd take the other two. But this way, with Webb in the picture . . . I just don't know."

"Thank you," Clint said.

"For what?"

"For being honest. Come on."

"Where are we going?"

"Let's just see where they're going. We'll start with that and move on from there."

They got out of their chairs and started down the street, the way Webb and the other three men had gone.

They didn't go far, though, only up to the sheriff's office. Clint and Maxim watched as Webb and one man entered while the other two stayed outside.

Clint and Maxim stopped several yards away from the sheriff's office and stepped into a doorway.

"Now, what do you suppose he's gonna do in there?" Maxim asked.

"Damned if I know," Clint said.

"Should we go in?"

"No," Clint said. "Let's wait out here and see what happens. We can check with the sheriff later, after Webb leaves."

"I gotta say," Maxim commented, shaking his head, "this is the last place I expected him to come."

"I gotta say," Clint answered, "me, too."

THIRTY-SEVEN

"It kind of surprised me, Sheriff, that you never came to see me."

Sheriff Slaten looked from Webb—whom he didn't know—to Jeff Bodine—whom he did—and then back at Jim Webb.

"Why's that?"

Webb was looking around the office, wrinkling his nose in distaste. He spoke without ever looking at Slaten, which the lawman recognized as a deliberate slight. The man was obviously trying to provoke him.

"Well, you're the law," Webb said. "Don't you check out the strangers who come to town?"

"You're not exactly a stranger, Webb."

Now Webb looked at him.

"You know me?"

"I know who you are," Slaten said, "and I know who you're friends with. You haven't caused any trouble in town—yet—so I haven't come to see you."

"Yet?" Webb asked. "You're expecting trouble from me, Sheriff?"

"I expect it will find you soon enough," Slaten said. "Tell me, what made you come to see me?"

"Talked about you with a mutual friend," Webb said.

147

"Oh? Who? Anson Blake?"

Webb shook his head.

"A little whore named Tina," he said, and he saw a muscle jump in Slaten's cheek. "She told me you're her boyfriend."

"That's right."

Webb whistled soundlessly and said, "Lucky man. I've had me some of that, you know. She's got about the hardest little body I ever came across—don't you think?"

Slaten counted to ten before answering.

"If you came here looking to provoke me into some kind of confrontation, Webb, you're wasting your time."

"Oh, that's right," Webb said, and then looked at Bodine, who had been standing off to the side silently until now. "His girlfriend did tell me he was a coward." He looked at Slaten. "I forgot."

Slaten gave Webb a tight smile.

"You'll have to do better than that, Webb," he said. "Tina wouldn't have told you that—and as far as her bein' with you—well, she's got to do a lot of things she doesn't like to make a livin'."

Now Webb gave Slaten a hard stare, one he expected to wither the lawman—but it didn't. Had Tina been wrong when she told him how easygoing the lawman was? Or had he been wrong to interpret "easygoing" to mean "cowardly"?

"Seems I might have pegged you wrong, Sheriff," he admitted slowly.

"Seems you might have," Slaten agreed.

"Well, then, let me tell you something straight-out," Webb said, leaning his palms on the sheriff's desk. "I am expectin' trouble. In fact, it's been doggin' my trail for months, and I plan on making my stand here. I'd advise you not to get in my way."

"I don't think I'll have to."

"Why not?"

"Seems I heard somethin' about your trouble," Slaten said. "Goes by the name Bass Reaves, don't it?"

Now a muscle in Webb's cheek twitched.

"Once he gets here I don't think I'll have to do anything . . . do you, Bodine?"

"Uh . . ." Bodine said, the first time he had spoken.

"No," Slaten said, "I don't think a man like Bass Reaves will need my help at all, do either of you?"

Webb stood up straight and stared at Slaten.

"Just remember what I said, Sheriff," he said. "Stay out of my way."

"That won't be a problem, Webb."

"See that it ain't," Webb said, wanting to have the last word before he walked out.

"Jeff," Slaten said, before the younger man could follow Webb.

"Yeah, Sheriff?"

"Is he payin' you enough to die with him?"

Bodine licked his lips.

"This feller Reaves, is he that good?"

"That's what I heard."

"But . . . he's a nigger."

"He's a federal marshal, Bodine," Slaten said. "Judge Parker don't hand those badges out to just anyone, you know."

Bodine licked his lips again.

"It don't matter," Bodine said. "Webb can take him."

"Maybe he will take him," Slaten said, "maybe after he kills you, though."

"Ain't gonna happen, Sheriff," Bodine said. "I'm too good with a gun."

"Jeff," Slaten said, "I think maybe you're gonna have a chance to prove that. What do you think?"

Bodine wiped his palms on his thighs and then left the office without answering.

Slaten sat back in his chair and frowned at the sweat

that had formed beneath his arms. Some of it had even
started to roll down his sides. He hoped he'd been able
to keep Webb from seeing it. The last thing he wanted
to show a man like Jim Webb was fear.

THIRTY-EIGHT

Clint and Maxim watched as Webb came out of the sheriff's office. The other man, Bodine, came out a few moments later, and got a tongue-lashing from Webb for it. That done, the four men started walking along the boardwalk—strolling, would have been more like it.

"They're just going for a walk," Clint said. "Let's go see the sheriff."

"Maybe I should follow them, anyway," Maxim said.

"And maybe we should just stick together, huh, Al?" Clint replied.

"Fine."

Maxim didn't like it, but he went along.

The sheriff looked up from his seat behind his desk and looked relieved to see them.

"Did you think Webb was coming back?" Clint asked.

"I was hoping not."

"Bad time?"

"He was pushing."

"You don't push?"

"I try not to," Slaten said, "but he was pushing hard. What can I do for you, Adams? Deputy? I see you're wearing your badge."

"That's right."

"Might not be a good idea right about now to do that," the local lawman said.

"Oh? Why's that?" Maxim asked.

"Webb seems to be looking for a fight."

"Before Reaves gets here?" Clint asked. "Why would he want to do that?"

"Maybe he just wants to get some practice in."

"We followed him here, Sheriff," Clint said. "He doesn't usually venture out of the saloon. Did he come just to push you?"

"Apparently," Slaten said. "I think he was testing me because . . . of something somebody told him."

"Like what?"

"Like maybe I'm a little easygoing."

Clint studied Slaten for a moment before replying.

"Webb is the kind of man who would hear 'cowardly' when someone said 'easygoing.' "

"You got it right."

"He got it wrong, I'd say."

"Thanks—but then why am I sweating so much?"

"Because you're human," Clint said. "Anybody'd sweat facing Webb, especially with somebody to back him up."

"I appreciate that," Slaten said, "from both of you. This'll interest you. He admitted he was setting a trap for Reaves."

"That just confirms what we've been thinking, but thanks," Clint said.

"He's on the street," Slaten said. "If you want to go get him I'll go with you."

"No reason for you to get involved, Sheriff," Clint said.

"You're worried that I couldn't pull my weight," Slaten said. "I don't blame you. You've never seen me before this week. You don't know what I can do."

Clint didn't bother telling the sheriff that he had the

same problem with Deputy Marshal Al Maxim.

"There's just no need for you to get involved, Sheriff," Clint said. "When Reaves gets here he and I and the deputy, here, will be more than able to handle it."

"I'm sure you will," Slaten said, "but this is my town and I have to have a say in what happens. With me along it'll be four against four."

"Well," Clint said, looking at Maxim, "you can't complain about those odds, can you?"

"Guess not."

"We'll come and get you, Sheriff, before we make a move."

"I appreciate that, Adams," Slaten said. "Mr. Webb needs to learn a thing or two about the local law in Colton."

THIRTY-NINE

By the time Clint and Maxim got back to the saloon, Webb and his friends were at their table. Webb didn't give them much attention until he suddenly saw the badge on Maxim's chest. He leaned forward and said something to the other three, who turned and looked at Maxim.

Clint and Maxim went to the bar and got a beer each from Leo.

"Okay," Maxim said, "now they know what I am, but they still don't know who you are."

"Well," Clint said, "if they ask Leo, he'll tell them . . . won't you, Leo?"

The big man said, "I will if you want me to, Mr. Adams."

"I think I do, Leo," Clint said. "I believe I do."

Clint and Maxim finished their beers, exchanged looks with the four men, and then left the saloon. Webb didn't go to the bar to talk to Leo, but he sent Bodine.

"Leo," Bodine said, "another beer."

Leo served it wordlessly.

"That feller with the deputy," Bodine said, taking hold of the beer mug.

"What about him?"

"You know who he is?"

"Yup."

Bodine waited, then said, "You gonna tell me?"

"You askin'?"

"Well, yeah, I'm askin', whataya think I'm doin', for Chrissake?"

"His name's Clint Adams."

"Ever seen him before?"

"Nope."

"What about the deputy?"

"Nope."

"That deputy, with the badge . . . was that badge for real?"

"I suppose so," Leo said. "He got it from Judge Parker."

"Has he been around—"

"Last coupla days or so."

"I didn't notice him."

"He wasn't wearin' the badge until today."

"Why not?"

Leo shrugged.

"Thanks, Leo."

Leo started cleaning the bar top with a towel and ignored Bodine.

Bodine walked back to the table and sat down with his fresh beer.

"Coulda brought us all fresh beer," Sam Ratliff complained.

"Shut up!" Webb said. "So?"

"Feller with the badge is one of Judge Parker's," Bodine said.

"Parker's," Webb said. "What the hell happened to Bass Reaves?"

Bodine shrugged.

"So we got us a white deputy instead of a nigger one," Ben Ratliff said. "So what?"

"We don't know that we got the white one instead of the black one," Webb said. "We may end up with both of them." He turned his attention back to Bodine. "How long has he been here?"

"Coupla days, Leo says."

"Why didn't anybody notice him?"

"Leo says he didn't have the badge on until today."

"Slick," Webb said. "Takin' a look around town before he shows everybody that he's a deputy."

"So what do we do about him?" Bodine asked.

"I don't know yet," Webb said. "Did you find out about that other fella?"

"Oh, yeah," Bodine said, "his name's Adams, Clint Adams."

"Adams?" Sam Ratliff said in a high voice.

"Clint Adams?" Ben Ratliff's voice went even higher.

"Yeah," Bodine said, "so?"

The Ratliffs looked at Webb.

"We didn't sign on to face no Clint Adams," Ben said.

"Shut up," Webb said. "Clint Adams." His eyes were shining.

"What's goin' on?" Bodine asked. "Who's Adams?"

"What are you, stupid?" Ben asked.

"You never heard of the Gunsmith?" Sam asked.

"Sure, I heard of the Gunsmith," Bodine said, "so what—wait a minute. This feller is *that* Clint Adams? The Gunsmith?"

"Now he gets it," Sam said to Ben, and they both shook their heads.

Bodine looked at Webb.

"You gotta let me take him, Webb," he said. "You gotta."

Webb snorted.

"He'd cut you down before you touched your gun."

"I'm good, Webb," Bodine said. "I been tellin' ya I'm good. I can take him."

The Ratliff boys laughed. Bodine stood up so fast he knocked his chair over. He drew his gun before either of the Ratliff boys knew what he was doing.

"Either one of you want to try me?" Bodine demanded, pointing his gun at them.

"Put the gun away, Bodine," Webb said.

"I'm just—"

"Put it away!"

Bodine hesitated, then holstered his gun, turned and stormed out of the saloon.

"That was a pretty good move, Webb," Sam said.

"Yeah, I didn't see him draw," Ben said.

"Maybe," Sam said, "you should let him take Adams."

"It was a good move," Webb admitted, "but this is the Gunsmith we're talkin' about, boys. You got any idea what that means?"

"Yeah," Ben said.

"He'll kill us," Sam said.

"But if we kill him," Webb said, "there's a big rep waiting for the one who actually kills him."

"You can have the big rep," Sam said.

"Ain't worth dying for," Ben said.

"Well, then, you boys get to take care of the marshal," Webb said, "and I'll take Adams."

"What about Bodine?" Ben asked.

"There's still the possibility Bass Reaves will show up," Webb said. "If he does, the kid can have him."

"That's fine with us," Sam said.

"Yeah, we'll take the white deputy," Ben said.

"He didn't look like much," Sam said.

"Boys," Webb said, standing up, "I'm gonna go to my room to do some thinkin'. If you see Marie, send her up, will ya?"

"How long you gonna be thinkin', Webb?" Sam asked.

"As long as it takes," Webb said, and went upstairs.

"How long is that?" Sam asked his brother.

Ben just shrugged.

FORTY

Clint and Maxim were having dinner in the hotel dining room when Anson Blake walked in. Clint was seated facing the door, and when Maxim saw the look on his face he turned around.

"What's he want?" he asked.

"I don't know," Clint said, "but he's on his way over, so we're about to find out."

"Mr. Adams," Blake said, "Deputy, do you fellas mind if I sit down? I don't mean to interrupt your meal, but . . . I have to talk to you."

"Have a seat, Mr. Blake," Clint said.

Thankfully, Blake sat down.

"We were about to order some pie and coffee. Would you care for some?"

"Sure," Blake said distractedly.

"Peach all right?"

"Fine."

Clint called the waiter over and ordered another pot of coffee and three pieces of peach pie.

"Now, what's on your mind, Mr. Blake?"

"Webb."

"What about him?"

"When do you think you'll be taking him out of here?" Blake asked.

"I don't know, Mr. Blake," Clint said. "We've kind of decided to wait for Marshal Reaves to arrive."

"And when will that be?"

"Should be any day now."

The waiter came with the pie and the coffee. Clint poured three cups, and then he and Maxim tucked into their pie while Blake ignored his.

"You don't know what it's like having him around all day long," Blake said. "It's a constant reminder of what . . . I used to be like, and I keep thinking . . . worrying. . . . wondering . . ."

"If he's going to drag you back into that life?" Clint finished for him.

Blake nodded.

"I don't think you have to worry, Mr. Blake," Clint said. "He probably would have tried to recruit you by now, if that was his intention."

"Do you really think so?"

"Yes, I do," Clint said, then looked at Maxim. "Don't you?"

"Huh?" Maxim said. "Oh, sure."

"See?"

"I hope you're right," Blake said.

"He couldn't make you do anything you didn't want to do," Maxim asked, "could he, Mr. Blake?"

Blake looked at Maxim, then looked away and stood up.

"Thanks for talking to me," he said, mostly to Clint, and then walked away.

"I guess maybe he could," Maxim said.

"Some men are not strong-willed, Al," Clint said, "although he was strong enough to quit outlawing and open his own business."

"Maybe he's just afraid of Webb."

"Yes," Clint said, "that could be it. Do you want his pie?"

Maxim shook his head.

"One slice is enough for me."

Clint reached for and captured Blake's pie and cut off a piece.

"So is that what we're doin'?" Maxim asked. "That's the big plan?"

"What is?"

"We're just gonna wait for Bass to get here?"

"If he's on the way, why not?" Clint asked. "Then we can get this over with together, and take him back to Fort Smith."

"What if he doesn't want to go?"

"And why wouldn't he, once this business with Webb is over?"

"I don't know," Maxim said, "maybe he'll just be stubborn about it."

"Well," Clint said, "I'm not going to try and force him to go back. I'll just deliver the judge's message and we can be on our way."

"So we're probably a day or two from ending this."

"That's my guess."

Maxim sipped some coffee then put his cup down and regarded Clint seriously.

"I got to thank you."

"For what?"

"For taking me along," he said. "I've learned a lot from you."

"Have you?"

"Yeah, I have," Maxim said. "I know I don't always listen, but I'm always watchin' and learnin'."

"You did all right, Al," Clint said. "You did fine."

"Now all I got left to prove is that I can watch your back in a fight."

"You know what?"

"What?"

"I hope you never get to prove it."

"That don't seem likely, does it?"

"No," Clint said, around the last chunk of Anson Blake's pie, "it doesn't."

FORTY-ONE

"Gotta be today," Al Maxim said, looking up and down the street.

"Sit down," Clint said. "You're going to make me jumpy."

They were sitting in front of the hotel and every five minutes Maxim would say, "Gotta be today," get up, look up and down the street, then sit down again . . . then start all over again.

"Sit down and stay down," Clint said. "He'll be here."

"How do you know?"

"If he's as good as everyone says," Clint said, "he'll be here."

"It'll be dark in half an hour," Maxim said.

"I would think that, being black," Clint said, "the dark would work in his favor."

Bass Reaves had pushed his horse as hard as he dared, and here he was, about a half an hour from dark, sitting astride his horse in front of a sign that said YOU ARE ENTERING THE TOWN OF COLTON with the population underneath it.

Well, if Jim Webb was there he wasn't included in

that number, so killing him wouldn't reduce it at all—
unless he had gotten himself some help. And knowing
Webb's reputation, Reaves was sure he had. Jim Webb
hadn't stayed alive this long by being foolish. He usually
didn't face anyone unless he had some guns backing him
up.

Bass started riding toward town, knowing that he was
heading into three, maybe four guns. He also knew that
the word hadn't gotten out about Webb being in Colton
by accident. He was reasonably sure that Jim Webb had
put the word out himself.

Bass Reaves was riding into a trap, and he knew it—
and he didn't care. His pistols, his rifle, and his shotgun
were all fully loaded; he was calm and collected and
ready to do what he had to do to bring Jim Webb in.

Colton was just ahead of him.

"I'll be a son of a bitch!" Maxim said.

Clint got up and moved up alongside him. He saw the
lone rider coming down the street just as dusk was fall-
ing in on them.

"That him?" Clint asked.

"That's him, all right," Maxim said. "Bass Reaves."

Reaves appeared to dwarf his horse, he was so big.
Clint was impressed that the man's size had not been
exaggerated.

"We'd better get to him before he does anything,"
Clint said, and they stepped off the boardwalk.

"Black man riding down the street!" someone in the
saloon shouted. "And he's wearin' a badge!"

Jim Webb looked around the table at Bodine and the
Ratliff brothers.

"This is it, boys," he said. "What we been waitin'
for. Are ya ready?"

"I'm ready," Bodine said.

"We ready?" Ben asked Sam.

"We're ready," Sam said.

Ben looked at Webb and said, "We're ready."

"Okay," Webb said, "here's how it works. Kid, you take Reaves."

"The nigger?" Bodine complained. "I wanted Adams."

"Adams is mine," Webb said.

"But it's the nigger's been trackin' you!" Bodine argued.

"Don't argue with me, boy!" Webb shot back. "I'm payin' for this party and I say you got the nigger marshal. Understand?"

Bodine looked away but said, "I understand."

"You Ratliff boys, you got the other deputy."

"Right," Sam said.

"I want him dead right off, understand?"

"We understand," Ben said.

"And I'll take care of Clint Adams," Webb said.

"What do we do after we killed the white deputy?" Ben asked. "Help you?"

"You just stay out of my way," Webb said. "See if Bodine needs any help."

Bodine's head snapped back as if he'd been slapped in the face.

"I ain't gonna need no help with no nigger!"

"Well, then, there's your answer, boys," Webb said to the Ratliffs. "Once you've killed the other deputy your job's done. You get to sit back and watch."

Webb took his gun from his holster, checked the loads, and slid it back.

"We goin' out?" Sam Ratliff asked.

"Naw," Webb said, "we're gonna make them come in after us."

FORTY-TWO

"I recognize the badge," Bass Reaves said, "but not the face."

Clint and Maxim had approached Reaves as he was dismounting outside the sheriff's office.

"You know me, Bass," Maxim said. "Al Maxim."

"Maxim?" Reaves frowned. "Yeah, Maxim. I do remember. What you doin' here, boy? And who's that you got wit' you?"

"Bass, this is Clint Adams."

Reaves obviously recognized the name.

"It's a pleasure," he said, extending his huge hand. Clint took it tentatively, but Reaves simply shook his hand without mangling it. A big, strong man who didn't have anything to prove.

"The judge tole me a lot about you."

"I've heard a lot about you, too, Bass," Clint said. "I have to say I'm surprised."

"At what?"

"Well, from what I heard about you these last couple of months I thought you'd be a raving lunatic by now."

Bass Reaves laughed and it sounded like thunder rumbling in his chest.

"Guess I was for a long time, there," Reaves said.

"The judge must think I gone plain loco."

"Some people think that," Maxim said.

"But not the judge," Clint added.

"Well, I guess I owe the man an explanation," Reaves said. "I'll give 'im one, too, soon as I think one up. For now you fellas should tell me why you're here."

"Well," Clint said, "we were tracking you and we ended up here."

"Heard about Webb, huh?"

"That's right."

"Why you trackin' me? The judge?"

Clint nodded.

"Wanted me to bring you a message."

"Which is?"

"Come on back."

"Webb here?"

Clint nodded.

"Be pretty silly, after everything that happened, to go back without him, wouldn't it?"

"It sure would."

"You agree?" Reaves asked Maxim.

"We're here to help."

"Where is Webb?"

"The saloon," Clint said.

"He got men wit' him?"

"Three," Maxim said.

"They any good?"

"We don't know," Maxim said. "One of them fancies himself a gun hand, but nobody knows if he's as good as he says he is."

"Guess we about to find out," Reaves said.

"The sheriff wants in on this, too," Clint said.

"I was gonna go in and talk to him. He inside?"

"He is."

"He all right?"

"He's a good man," Clint said, "but I don't know how he'll be in a fight."

"Reckon we'll find that out, too, huh?" Reaves said.

"Reckon we will," Maxim said.

"Might as well go in and talk to the man," Reaves said. "Webb's waited this long, he can wait a little longer."

The three of them mounted the boardwalk and entered the sheriff's office.

"I'll be—" Bodine said, turning away from the window. "They gone into the sheriff's office."

"All three?" Webb asked.

"Yep."

"What are they goin' in there for?" Ben asked.

"This fight might be even, boys," Webb said. "Anybody know what kind of man the sheriff is in a fight?"

Bodine shook his head. The Ratliff boys looked at each other and did the same.

"Then I guess one of you boys will have to take care of him," Webb said, looking at the brothers, "and one will have to take the young deputy."

"Yeah," Ben said, looking puzzled, "but which one?"

"I don't like the plan," Maxim said.

"I think it has merit," Clint said.

"I think it keeps me on the outside," Maxim complained.

"In case any of them get by us," Bass Reaves pointed out. "Makes sense to have somebody on the outside."

"Then why can't it be the sheriff?" Maxim asked.

" 'Cause I got another job for him," Reaves said.

"I still don't like it," Maxim said. "Clint could stay outside."

"Now, boy," Reaves said, "was I to go into a fight with you backin' me and Clint Adams waitin' outside what would people say about me?"

Maxim frowned, then admitted, "They'd be sayin' you were a danged fool."

"Can't have them sayin' that about me, now, can we?" Bass asked.

FORTY-THREE

"They're comin'!" Bodine shouted.

That's all the other men in the saloon had to hear. Suddenly, they stampeded toward the door and Bodine had to scramble to get out of the way or be trampled.

Outside Clint, Bass Reaves, and Maxim also had to move quickly to avoid being knocked over. They waited until the last man had come out of the saloon, then approached it again. It was now fully dark out.

"Webb!" It was decided that Reaves would do the talking. Tracking Webb for months gave him that right. "You got one chance to come out with your hands up and come back to Fort Smith to answer for your crimes."

"Fuck you, nigger!" Webb called out. "Come in and get me."

They heard some noise and knew what it was—at least, Clint and Bass knew. The men inside had tossed over some tables to use as cover.

Reaves looked at Clint, who nodded. They each knew what their moves were going to be once they were inside. Since Clint had already been in the saloon he was able to describe it for Reaves, who now knew what the inside looked like as if he'd been there himself. Bar to the left, tables to the right. Clint was going to go in and left, using the bar for cover. Reaves was going in and right, turning over a table for his own cover.

"You other men inside," Reaves called. "You got one chance to come out."

No answer.

"They ain't comin' out," Reaves said. "It woulda been nice for them to surrender."

"Oh, well," Clint said, "how often does plan A work?"

"Ready for plan B?" Bass asked.

"I'm ready."

They both looked at Maxim.

"What do I have to be ready for?" he asked. "You fellas are havin' all the fun."

"Just be alert," Clint said. "If my past experience is any indication, somebody's going to be coming out one of these windows. Make sure it's not me or Bass before you shoot, huh?"

"I know, I know."

Pssst.

They all heard the sound and turned to look. Leo, the bartender, was coming from the side of the saloon, beckoning to them. Clint went over.

"What is it, Leo?"

"I come out the back," the big bartender said. "There are four of them, and they got two tables overturned for cover."

"All of them behind the tables?"

Leo nodded.

"Thanks, Leo. Where's your boss?"

"He's in his office," Leo said. "He won't come out."

"It's best if he doesn't," Clint said. "Why don't you get away from here, Leo, and come back when the shooting stops."

"Good luck," Leo said, and he took off down the street.

Clint returned to Reaves and told him what the bartender had said.

"Like we thought," he said. "Wait a minute."

He walked to his horse, ejected the shells from his shotgun, took some different shells from his saddlebags and loaded them, then returned to the front of the saloon.

"Ready?" he asked.

"I'm ready," Clint said.

There was a moment of silence and then Maxim said, "Yeah, yeah, I'm ready, too."

"The sheriff must be in position," Reaves said. "Let's go."

He and Clint mounted the boardwalk and edged their way to the bat-wing doors.

"One . . ." Reaves said.

"Two . . ." Clint said.

They both said, "Three!" at the same time and charged into the saloon.

FORTY-FOUR

Clint went in low, beneath the swinging doors, and then cut left to take cover behind the bar. After the darkness outside it was pretty bright in the room. He fired once, but knew he wouldn't hit anything. It was just to get their attention, and to give him time to adjust to the light.

Bass Reaves went in high and a bullet whizzed by him, taking just a small nick from his ear as it went. He cut right and overturned a table right by the window to use as cover.

Webb and his men were firing their guns as quickly as they could. Lead was taking chunks out of the table Bass was using for cover, and also chewing up the corner of the bar. Reaves looked over at Clint and shouted above the din, "Get ready. I'm gonna get you a clear shot."

Clint didn't know what Bass was going to do, but he was ready. Abruptly, the big black man stood up, pointed his shotgun, and fired both barrels.

The extra heavy gauge ammunition struck one of the tables Webb and his men were using as cover and split the damned thing right in half!

Clint stood up and fired. The two men who had been

177

behind that table were stunned. Wood chips stung their faces and it was a miracle they had escaped direct injury from the shotgun blast. However, one of them didn't escape for long as Clint's shot buried itself in the man's chest.

Reaves dropped his shotgun, drew one of his handguns and shot the other man.

Now there was only Webb and Bodine behind the other table.

"This ain't the way you said it would be!" Bodine accused.

"You're on your own, boy," Webb said.

At that point the back door opened and the sheriff stepped in. Webb shot him in the shoulder, spinning him around and knocking him to the ground.

"Finish him!" he shouted at Bodine.

"What are you—" Bodine started, but Webb was already moving.

Bodine turned to look at the sheriff, who was down but not out. He still held his gun, and before Bodine could do anything to live up to all the bragging he'd done for years about how good he was with a gun, Sheriff Mark Slaten killed him.

Webb had taken off running down the center of the room. Both Clint and Bass turned to fire at him, but then Clint held a hand up to Bass, stopping him. The black man knew what he was doing and held his fire.

Just as Clint had warned Al Maxim, Jim Webb hurled himself through one of the saloon windows. He hit the boardwalk outside and rolled into the street, came up on one knee facing Al Maxim.

"Got the sand for this, boy?" Webb asked. His eyes weren't used to the darkness. He couldn't make out the figure's face, but he assumed it was the other deputy.

If Maxim had hesitated to answer the question he would have been dead. As it was he heeded Clint's warning about the window and was ready. He fired once, striking Webb in the neck, but not killing him. Starting to choke on his own blood Webb brought his gun up.

Clint had stepped out through the bat-wing doors and when he saw the two men he shouted at Maxim, "Again, damn it! Again!"

Maxim fired a second time. This time the bullet hit Webb in the center of the chest, knocking him onto his back. It was a toss-up as to whether he'd drown in his own blood or his heart would stop from the damage done by the bullet.

He was dead in minutes—and it didn't matter which one killed him.

Bass Reaves came out as Clint and Maxim were leaning over Webb. He was supporting the sheriff easily with one arm, as if the man weighed nothing. Light from the broken window framed Webb's body perfectly.

"Sheriff ain't hurt bad, but he needs a doctor," Reaves said. "The others are dead."

"So's Webb," Clint said. "Maxim killed him."

"Reward's yours, then."

"Jesus," Maxim said, "you're the one been tracking him for months."

"Don't matter to me," Reaves said. "I just wanted him stopped. He's stopped."

"You okay?" Clint asked, seeing that the right side of Reaves's neck and face was bloody.

"Fine," he said, "just took a bite out of my ear."

"Let's get the sheriff to the doctor," Clint said.

FORTY-FIVE

The next morning Clint, Maxim, and Bass Reaves had breakfast in the hotel dining room. If the staff objected to a black man eating there, no one said a word. The other diners sneaked looks at the big black marshal but likewise remained silent and ate their breakfast.

"Are you heading back to Fort Smith today, Bass?" Clint asked.

"Sure am," Reaves said. "I been on Webb's trail for a long time, outta my head for most of it, though I don't exactly know why. I expect maybe I need me some rest."

"Rest ain't a bad idea," Maxim agreed.

"What you got to rest about?" Reaves asked. "You a young man."

"Young men get tired, too, ya know."

"What about you, Clint?" Reaves asked. "You going back to Fort Smith to see the judge?"

"No reason for me to go back," Clint said. "I did what I said I would, I delivered his message. I guess you could deliver one for me."

"What's that?" Reaves asked.

181

"Tell him next time he wants somebody to chase after you," Clint said, "get somebody else."

Reaves laughed.

"I'll tell him that," he said. "I surely will."

Watch for

DEAD MAN'S BLUFF

203rd novel in the exciting GUNSMITH series
from Jove

Coming in December!